LINDA TURNER

His Wanted Woman

Romantic
SUSPENSE

 **SILHOUETTE BOOKS**

Recycling programs for this product may not exist in your area.

ISBN-13: 978-0-373-27655-4

HiS WANTED WOMAN

"Don't."

She'd meant to sound firm and cool, yet her voice was anything but. Horrified, she ordered herself to put some space between them. Her feet, however, refused to move. And it was all Patrick's fault. If he would just stop touching her…

Unable to take her eyes from him, she reached blindly for his hand. "I'm fine," she said huskily.

But instead of pushing him away, she clung to him like a lifeline.

The feel of her fingers wrapped around his caught Patrick off guard. This was crazy. Just that morning, she'd been a suspect, and now all he could think about was the softness of her skin, her mouth…and kissing her.

Dear Reader,

Before I started writing, I worked for the FBI in Washington, D.C., and loved it. So going back to D.C. thirty years later to research this book was almost like going home. A lot has changed since the late '70s: the street in front of the White House is closed to traffic and the FBI no longer gives tours. When I was working at the Bureau, all you had to do to take a tour of the White House—even a candlelit one at Christmas—was get in line.

Those days are gone, but Washington is still a wonderful city, and steeped in history. My kind of place! That's why I love Mackenzie and Patrick's story so much. If I ever had a bookstore, I would want it to look just like Sloan Antiquarian Books and Maps. Enjoy!

Linda Turner

Selected books by Linda Turner

Silhouette Romantic Suspense

LINDA TURNER

began reading romances in high school and began writing them one night when she had nothing else to read. She's been writing ever since. Single and living in Texas, she travels every chance she gets, scouting locales for her books.

I owe special thanks to Kelly Maltagliati and Matthew Elliott, who are both special agents with the Office of the Inspector General of the National Archives and Records Administration, and Mitchell Yockelson, an investigative archivist with the Office of the Inspector General. I would also like to thank Harry Husberg with the Ft. Worth Police Department for his advice on police procedures. Thank you all for your expertise and ideas.

Prologue

The old tavern was packed with St. Patrick's Day revelers who were loud, boisterous and in the mood to party. Rushing inside, his black, wavy hair and sharp features glistening with the damp mist that had socked in Washington, D.C., Patrick O'Reilly wasn't surprised to find his two brothers already seated at their favorite table, right next to the fireplace, where a roaring fire took the chill off the air. They both worked just around the corner from the bar and didn't even have to move their cars. He, on the other hand, had been working a case across town and had been caught in traffic.

Devin spied him first as he made his way through the crowd and grinned, though there was little amusement in his steel-blue eyes. "It's about damn time you got here. We started without you," he said, and raised his Guinness in a salute.

"We ordered you one," Logan added. "Devin didn't think you were coming, so he drank it for you."

"Hey, it was getting warm," he said, defending himself. "Here. You can have mine."

"No, thanks." Patrick chuckled. "I'll get my own."

Signaling the waitress for another beer, he sank into the wooden chair between his brothers and lifted a dark brow. "Well? Did you bring them?"

Devin and Logan didn't have to ask what he was talking about. They both pulled out a single piece of paper and tossed it onto the table, then waited for Patrick to do the same. Reaching into his inner coat pocket, he produced his own document and added it to the two on the table.

"That's a pretty sorry sight," Logan retorted as the waitress delivered another round to their table. "Three brothers. Three divorces, all within six months of each other. Who could have guessed?"

"You should have," Patrick drawled, "at least when it came to yourself. You never believed in marriage anyway. How you let Jan talk you into walking down the aisle, I'll never know."

"Yeah," Devin said. "You always said marriage was unnatural. Then the next thing we know, you're planning a damn wedding."

His green eyes twinkling ruefully, Logan shrugged. "What can I say? It was temporary insanity, and I learned my lesson the hard way."

"You weren't the only one," Patrick said grimly. "At least you didn't fall for a liar.

"I saw that look," he added when his brothers exchanged speaking glances. "You two are as bad as Mom. Just because I'm never going to get married again doesn't mean I'm bitter. I'm just not stupid."

Grinning, Logan held up his hands in surrender. "Hey, you won't get an argument out of me. Our mama didn't raise any idiots."

"Just a bunch of cops who have bad taste in women," Devin added, chuckling. "I think she'd rather have idiots."

Patrick laughed. "Too bad. She's stuck with us." Raising his beer, he clicked glasses with his brothers.

"To the three stooges," Devin said with twinkling eyes.

"Speak for yourself," Logan tossed back. "To the three musketeers."

"To never getting married again," Patrick said.

"Amen," his brothers said.

And without further ceremony, they each picked up their marriage licenses and, on the two-year anniversary of their divorces, tossed them into the fire. Within seconds, the licenses…and the relationships of the past…went up in smoke.

Chapter 1

"Geez, Mac, how do you stand all this?" Stacy Green sniffed, wrinkling her nose at the dust she had stirred as she helped sort stacks of old documents and maps that looked like they hadn't been touched in years. "I know you said your dad really let the place go over the last couple of years, but it's going to take you decades to get this all cleaned up."

In the process of changing the seasonal display in the shop's bow window from Thanksgiving to Christmas, Mackenzie Sloan said, "Bite your tongue. It's not that bad."

"Yeah, right." Stacy snorted. "And I'm the Queen Mother."

"I'm making progress," she insisted, but as she looked around at the antique bookstore her father had left her when he died unexpectedly three months ago, Mackenzie had to admit that Stacy was right. The place was a mess. In spite of the fact that she'd been cleaning and trying to organize the shop since the day after her father's funeral, it was still little more than barely controlled chaos.

Guilt tugged at her, bringing the sting of tears to her eyes. "I should have come home more often—"

"Don't you dare blame yourself!" Stacy, her oldest friend and fiercest protector, immediately jumped to her defense. "You were working a crazy schedule and spending every spare moment on your master's. Not to mention trying to have a life with a man you loved! When would you have come home? Between two and three in the morning? You were in California, for God's sake, not across the street!"

"I know," she sighed. "That's why Dad came to see me instead. And he acted like everything was fine. I didn't have a clue he was sick."

"He didn't want you to know, Mac. You would have quit school and come home and he would have hated that. You were so close to finishing. He didn't want you to give that up for him."

"And the irony of it is, Hugh and I broke up and I came home anyway," she said with a grimace of a smile.

"*After* you got your master's," Stacy pointed out.

"True," she agreed. But by then, it had been too late for her father. "At least Dad died knowing I was able to finish school." Shaking off her sadness, she forced a smile. "He was a great dad. And in spite of the condition of the shop, he left me a business I love."

"I'm just worried you're working yourself to death," Stacy said, frowning. "I hardly see you anymore. You're working night and day. I bet you don't even remember the last time you had a date."

"There are plenty of men in my life—"

"Oh, really? Name one."

"Lincoln…Washington…Stonewall Jackson…"

Stacy gave her a reproving look. "Cute, smarty-pants. This is serious. I'm concerned."

"I'm fine."

"You need to let me introduce you to Baxter Townsend. If I wasn't married and crazy about my lover boy—"

"Not to mention seven months pregnant," Mackenzie said dryly, grinning as she patted her friend's extended tummy. "Or are you forgetting about my goddaughter?"

A tender smile curved Stacy's mouth as she placed a hand over her stomach. "How could I forget her? The little stinker kicks me all night long. I think she's going to be a soccer player."

"Then she'll have to get that gene from John. You haven't got an athletic bone in your body."

Grimacing, Stacy grinned. "Too sweaty. But you like sports. You and Baxter would get along great. He played tennis in college."

"Stace—"

"He's never been married," she added, "and makes a ton of money. He's a—"

"No."

"At least meet him. You two are perfect for each other."

Mackenzie rolled her eyes. The last man Stacy had claimed was perfect for her and had actually introduced her to had turned about to be an alcoholic with a temper. "Do I need to remind you of Gus Dole?"

Stacy had the grace to wince. "Ouch! Okay, so I screwed up with Gus. And now that I think about it, you probably wouldn't be crazy about Baxter—he can be kind of pompous. But you're fading away in this shop, turning to dust just like your father's books and old maps. You've got to get out of here!"

"I do," she argued. "I go somewhere nearly every weekend."

"To memorabilia shows." Stacy sniffed. "Where you meet dusty old men who are pushing eighty and only interested in one thing—buying something that belonged to Washington or Jefferson or God knows who else. Dammit, Mac, you're twenty-eight years old! When your father left you the business, he didn't intend for you to bury yourself in it."

"Maybe not," she agreed. "But you said yourself this place is a mess. Can you think of any man you know who would want to take on this and me? He'd have to be crazy."

"Not crazy," Stacy retorted, grinning. "Just a confident, good-looking hunk who likes to read about Thomas Jefferson and John Adams instead of girly magazines. How hard can that be to find?"

"Yeah, right." Mackenzie laughed. "When you find him, let me know."

The door to the shop opened then, and, as always, a John Philip Sousa march began to softly play throughout the shop and apartment upstairs. As the music grew progressively louder, Mackenzie, as always, laughed.

John Philip Sousa had been born in Washington, D.C., but that wasn't the only reason her father had chosen a Sousa march for the musical alarm he'd installed years ago. He'd had a tendency to get caught up in his work and lose track of what was going on around him and he'd needed something to jar him back to attention when someone walked through the front door. Even now, in her mind's eye, she could see him jump as the cymbals crashed loudly, reminding him he had a customer.

Beside her, Stacy glanced at the customer who strolled in, only to immediately smile with quick interest. "Oh, goodness, what do we have here? I think I'm in love."

"Stop that!" Mackenzie hissed as her own eyes roamed over the customer who looked like something out of one of her fantasies. Tall, dark and handsome— there was no other way to describe him. With dimples that framed either side of his mouth and a boyish glint in his green eyes, he had *trouble* written all over him. Mackenzie took one look at that long, lean body and fantastic face and forgot to breathe.

Stacy, on the other hand, had no such trouble. "Well, hello," she said with a grin. "Aren't you the cutest thing? I'll bet you're a history major, aren't you?"

Caught off guard, he laughed. "As a matter of fact, I am."

"And you're a Civil War buff."

"Stacy," Mackenzie warned.

"I'm just asking," she said innocently.

"I've been known to spend days at Gettysburg studying strategy," he admitted. "Is that a problem?"

"Not at all," Stacy said before Mackenzie could say a word. "There's just something about history majors—"

Shooting her friend a quelling glance, Mackenzie said, "Is there something in particular you were looking for or would you just like to look around?"

"I'll look around," he said with a wicked grin and a wink at Stacy. "Thanks."

"Civil War books and maps are upstairs," Mackenzie told him. "Just let me know if you need some help."

"You'll be the first person I call," he promised and headed up the stairs.

The second he was out of sight, Mackenzie whirled on Stacy. "What are you doing?"

"Just having a little fun." She chuckled. "And you should, too. An honest-to-goodness hunk just walked through the door and what do you do? Treat him just like one of your regular customers. You haven't had anyone under sixty-five walk through that door since your dad died. What were you thinking?!"

"He's a customer—"

"No! He's a good-looking man who doesn't happen to have a ring on his finger, in case you didn't notice."

She'd noticed, all right, but she would have cut out her tongue before she admitted it. "I don't know what you're talking about."

"Bull!" Stacy laughed. "Tell that to someone who hasn't known you since you were four. But I'm not going to harass you," she added with a grin. "I'm meeting John for dinner, so I've got to go." Giving her a quick hug, she headed for the door. "Don't do anything I wouldn't do."

"Stacy!"

Laughing, she disappeared out the door with a teasing wave.

Five seconds later, Mackenzie heard a step on the stairs and whirled to find the *"hunk,"* as Stacy described him, standing on the landing. Mortified, she could have sunk right through the floor. Had he heard what Stacy said?

Mackenzie only had to see the glint of humor in his eyes to know that he'd heard every word. She was, she decided, going to hang Stacy by her ears the next time she saw her.

Heat climbing in her cheeks, she lifted her chin and met his gaze head-on. "Did you see anything you like?"

His lips twitched. "That depends. For the right price, I could take just about everything in your shop home with me."

Studying him through narrowed blue eyes, she told herself he surely wasn't including her in "everything." But there was something about the man's confidence that told her there was little he wouldn't dare.

"What, in particular, were you interested in?"

He shrugged. "Oh, I don't know. Let's start small. I noticed you had a framed letter from one of the soldiers at Valley Forge. What's the price tag on that?"

"You won't like it."

She watched as he literally and figuratively rolled up his sleeves and braced himself. "Try me."

"A thousand."

"*What?!* That's outrageous!"

"For an original piece of American history?" she

scoffed. "I don't think so. I can get twice that much on eBay."

"eBay? Bite your tongue!"

His reaction didn't surprise her. Many serious collectors didn't believe in buying anything they couldn't see and examine before money exchanged hands. "I have to make a sale where I can. If you're not interested—"

Not fooled by her ploy, he grinned. "You're damn good at this."

"I come from a long line of horse traders," she said, "and I have a feeling you do, too."

"I'm Irish," he said simply. "It's in the blood. So how about a trade?"

Wary, she frowned. "What kind of trade?"

For an answer, he pulled out a yellowed, folded piece of paper in a sealed Ziploc bag. "Just a little something I picked up years ago that you might be interested in," he told her casually.

Curiosity threatening to get the best of her, Mackenzie just barely resisted the urge to reach for it. "If you're wanting to trade even-steven," she warned, "you need to know that I don't usually do that. You'd have to offer something pretty phenomenal for me to agree to an equal trade."

Amused, he said, "You're assuming your letter is more valuable than my map."

Mackenzie's ears perked up at that. She loved maps—and so did her customers—but she had no intention of letting him know that. "A map, huh? I don't know about that. Most of my customers are more interested in first edition books."

Not the least bit worried, he held the Ziploc bag out to her. "You might want to look at it before you make a decision," he told her. "It's a map of Gettysburg hand-drawn by General Lee. There are also notes in the margin containing his field strategy."

Already reaching for it, Mackenzie looked up sharply. "This is the General's Map?"

A cool smile touched his lips. "So you've heard of it."

Heard of it? Of course she'd heard of it! Who hadn't? It had disappeared soon after the Battle of Gettysburg and hadn't been seen since. There'd been rumors that it had been owned over the years by everyone from P. T. Barnum to the Rockefellers to a Saudi prince who was a Civil War collector. If the map was authentic, how had it ended up in the hands of the man before her?

"Go ahead," he said when she gave him a wary look. "Take a look at it. Tell me what you think. I already know what it's worth, of course. I'm wondering if you do."

Another dealer might have been insulted by his words, but Mackenzie didn't need to defend herself to anyone. Her master's was in American history, and she'd worked in the business of buying antique docu-ments and rare books for more than half her life. If the map was genuine, there was no doubt that it would be worth a small fortune.

Questions—and doubts—tugging at her, she took the map and moved to the reading table that was situated in front of the fireplace. Armed with the magnifying glass she carried on a cord around her neck, she care-fully pulled the map out of the Ziploc and unfolded it under the light in the center of the table. The paper was yellowed with age, the bold, scrawled notes in the margin still legible despite the fact that the map was, reportedly, nearly a hundred and fifty years old.

Mackenzie loved old maps, but she knew better than most that they weren't always what they appeared to be. Forgery was a serious problem in her business... and so was theft.

"Where did you say you got this?" she asked casually as she put her magnifying glass to the map.

"I didn't," he said just as casually. "It belonged to a friend of mine. He's had a hell of a lot of bad luck lately—he got divorced, then lost his job when the company he worked for shipped out to India. Last week, he lost his house."

"So he was desperate and sold a family heirloom," she concluded. "Or was he a collector? Maybe I know him."

"A collector?" he scoffed, laughing shortly. "Not hardly. He's into motorcycles and NASCAR. His grandfather left him the map years ago—he was just hanging on to it for a rainy day. He doesn't even have money for an apartment. It's not just raining—it's a damn hurricane."

"I see." Continuing to examine the map, she saw, all right, more than he wanted her to. His story had lie written all over it and didn't make a bit of sense. If the real owner had been saving it for a rainy day, the last thing he would have done was sell it to a friend when he was in desperate straits. Instead, he would have taken it to Sotheby's or another high-dollar auction house that would have advertised it and gotten him a fortune for the sale.

If, she silently amended, the map was authentic. Looking at it under the glass, she had to admit that she had her doubts. There were file notations from the U.S. War Department on the back of the document that didn't quite look right. And while that might not be enough to indicate that the map was a forgery, the fact that the present owner and previous one were strangers to her made her very uneasy. The people who collected the more valuable Civil and Revolutionary War memorabilia were a relatively small group. Everybody knew everybody else, for the most part, especially in the Washington, D.C./Virginia/Maryland area. And she had never laid eyes on the man standing before her.

If she had, she certainly would have remembered him. With his sharp green eyes, wavy black hair and chiseled good looks, he wasn't the kind of man a woman forgot.

Especially when he smiled. Those dimples of his were downright dangerous.

Suddenly realizing she was staring at the sensuous curve of his lips, she stiffened. What was she doing? She didn't care how good-looking the man was, he may very well be trying to selling her a forged map!

Deliberately pulling her attention back to the document spread out before her, she was tempted to buy it just so he couldn't walk out with it and sell it to someone who might mistakenly think it was authentic. Just the idea of giving money to a crook for what was nothing but a forgery, however, outraged her.

Think! she told herself fiercely. There had to be something she could do. If she told him she had a customer who might be interested, but she couldn't get an answer from him for at least three days, that would give her time to research not only the legitimacy of the map, but any recent news about it.

But even as the words hovered on her tongue, she knew she couldn't let him walk out with the map with the promise that he would return in three days. The odds were he wouldn't, and the map—if it really was authentic—would be lost forever. She had to do something now!

The decision made, she set down her magnifying glass with a snap and looked up at him with narrowed eyes that missed little. "What'd you say your name was?"

"I didn't," he replied easily. "But you can call me O'Reilly."

Making no attempt to hide her suspicions, she said, "Where'd you really get the map?"

"I beg your pardon?"

"And well you should," she retorted. "You're lying through your teeth and we both know it. The map, if it's real—and I have my doubts about that—has file notes on the back. So tell me, O'Reilly, where did the map really come from? Did you steal it or create it?"

He didn't even blink. "No."

"It's not stolen?"

"No."

"So it's a fake," she concluded.

"I didn't say that."

No, it's not stolen. No, it's not a fake. That's all he said…just *no*. Frustrated, Mackenzie couldn't believe his audacity. No explanation, no nothing. Snatching up the map, she held it out to him. "I don't believe you. Take it and get out. I don't deal with thieves or forgers."

Patrick had to give her credit. Talk about the pot calling the kettle black! He almost believed her. It was her eyes, he decided. They were big and blue and bright with indignation. How could a woman with eyes like that, with the face of an angel, possibly be a thief?

Watch it, a voice in his head growled. *If you're not careful, you're going to become obsessed with the woman.*

It was the case he was obsessed with, he told himself, not the woman. But he'd been watching every move she made for the last three weeks without her even being aware of it, and it was her face he saw when he investigated the sales on eBay. It was her smile he saw through the lens of his camera when he set up surveillance and watched everyone who walked through the front door of her shop for days on end. And at night, when he left the office and the case behind and went home, it was the woman herself he couldn't get out of his head when he crawled into bed.

He shouldn't have come here today, he silently acknowledged. And he certainly shouldn't have approached her without another agent with him to witness what went down. It was totally against procedure.

But the more he investigated Mackenzie Sloan, the more she confused him. She looked like a modern-day Princess Diana, for God's sake, and there wasn't a hint of scandal attached to her name. So how was she up to her pretty little ears in the sale of stolen antiquities? Frustrated, he'd been on the way home from work when he'd decided on the spur of the moment to stop by her shop and confront the lady face-to-face.

In for a penny, in for a pound, he thought, and

mocked, "You don't deal with thieves, huh? That might be easier to believe if you weren't one yourself."

Surprised, she gasped, "What are you talking about? I've never stolen anything in my life!"

"Oh, really? Then what would you call this?" And reaching into his pocket, he pulled out a second yellowed piece of paper.

Watching her closely, Patrick saw her eyes flare at the sight of a playbill from Ford's Theatre that was given to theatergoers the night of Lincoln's assassination. It was her nearly soundless gasp, however, that told him everything he needed to know. He wasn't surprised she recognized the stolen document. She should have.

She was the one who'd sold it to a private collector on eBay.

Chapter 2

Outraged, Mackenzie couldn't believe he was serious. "Excuse me?"

"You heard me," he said coolly. "If you've never stolen anything in your life, what would you call this? This was Lincoln's playbill the night he was shot."

"I know what it is," she huffed, "but I don't where you got the idea it was stolen. My father—"

"Stole it from the National Archives," he cut in.

"He did not!"

"And you sold it on eBay to a private collector," he continued. "So save the outrage and pretend innocence for someone who appreciates it. You recognized the playbill the second I showed it to you."

Mackenzie didn't deny it. "Of course I recognize it," she retorted, stung. "I inherited the business from my dad three months ago and I've been selling a lot of the excess inventory. I sold the playbill last month."

"So you admit it," he said smugly.

"I admit that I sold it," she said, irritated, "not that it was stolen. It couldn't have possibly been. My father bought the playbill from a descendant of a congressman who was at Ford's Theatre the night of the assassination."

"How do you know that for sure? Did your father investigate this so-called descendant? What's his name? Could he prove continuous ownership of the playbill? Where did your father meet him?"

He threw questions at her like bullets, grilling her like she was some kind of ax murderer when *he* was the one who had some explaining to do. Indignant, she snapped, "You've got a hell of nerve! My father was in this business for thirty years, and he had an impeccable reputation. Don't you dare stand here in *his* shop and slam him!

"And you're a fine one to talk," she added, glaring at him. "Speaking of where things come from, where did you get your map, mister? From some sleazy forger? Oh, yeah, I know it's a fake. My father taught me how to spot a phony when I was eight years old."

And with no more warning than that, she reached over and snatched up the map he'd laid on the counter when he pulled the playbill from the inside pocket of his jacket. "I'll take that, thank you very much. I'm not going to stand by and let you sell that to some poor unsuspecting schmuck who's got *sucker* stamped on his forehead. Now get out of here before I call the police."

He studied her with real admiration in his eyes. "You're good," he told her, his smile mocking. "The

outrage in your voice, that spark of anger in your eyes—
I've got to tell you, sweetheart, you're just about the best
I've ever seen. But you know what? I'm going to call
your bluff."

"It's not a bluff! And don't call me sweetheart!"

"Then go ahead and call the police," he taunted.
"And while you're at it, make sure you tell the dis-
patcher that I'm a federal agent for the Archives."

When he slapped his badge down on the counter in
front of her, Mackenzie couldn't take her horrified gaze
off it. This couldn't be happening, she thought, dazed.
There had to be a mistake. She'd never taken anything
that didn't belong to her, and neither had her father. And
every time she purchased an antique document or rare
book, she checked the chain of ownership…just as her
father had. There was no way either one of them could
have bought stolen documents.

"I don't know where you got your information," she
said flatly, "but you're wrong. My father would never do
such a thing, and neither would I. You've made a mistake."

"You think so? Then maybe you can explain why two
dozen documents were missing after your dad did
research at the Archives. And don't tell me he never did
research there. I've got the records to prove it."

Cold dread tightened Mackenzie's stomach into a
hard knot of nerves. He was so sure, so cocky, but if he
thought he was going to make her doubt her own father
so easily, he could think again.

"And that's your proof?" she challenged. "My father
did research at the Archives for decades. So have thousands of other people over the years. When exactly did

one of the Archives's employees discover documents were missing?"

"Two months ago."

"A month *after* my father died?"

"We believe the papers went missing during your father's visit to the Archives last year."

"You *believe?*" she said sharply. "You aren't sure?"

He shrugged. "The Archives has billions of documents. It's impossible to inventory them all."

"Then how do you know my father took anything if you don't even know what really belongs to the Archives?"

"We have documents connected to the missing items," he retorted. "Responses to letters, maps from the same military campaigns. Trust me, we know."

"Trust you?" she scoffed. "I don't think so. Not when you're making accusations and you don't even know for sure that the missing documents were in the files at the time my father did his research. They could have been stolen years before that."

"True," he agreed. "The only problem with that is you sold all of the missing items on eBay. So where did you get them if your father didn't steal them?"

Caught in the trap of his mocking eyes, Mackenzie couldn't believe he was serious. Her father was the best man she'd ever known. He'd taught her more about history than any college professor she'd ever had, and there was nothing he respected more than the rare books and documents he bought and sold to collectors all over the world. He would never have stolen the very things he loved, then sold them to an unsuspecting buyer. He wasn't that kind of man.

And yes, she did sell the playbill Agent O'Reilly taunted her with, as well as the other documents he claimed her father had stolen. There were no file notes, however, nothing to indicate that the documents were anything but privately owned. So why would she suspect anything? None of this made any sense.

Except that your father was doing research at the Archives, an irritating voice whispered in her ear. *If he'd wanted to steal something, the opportunity was there.*

Cold chills raced down her arms at the thought. *No!* she silently cried, drowning out the doubt that suddenly pulled at her like a molester in the night. Her father knew he was dying…and that any theft at the Archives would turn up long after he died. He had to know that if he really stole something, she would be the one to take the fall for him. He loved her. He wouldn't have done that to her. He would have sold his soul first.

Fighting the need to cry just at the thought, she lifted her chin and met the agent's gaze head on. "My father wasn't a thief. I don't care what records you found or what misguided conclusions you've come to. You're wrong. I handled every one of those documents. There was nothing on them to indicate they were the property of the U.S. government."

"So where did they come from if they weren't stolen?" he demanded. "Show me your records."

She didn't even blink. "Where's your search warrant?"

Patrick had to give her credit. She was quick. And he'd made the rookie mistake of letting his curiosity get the best of him when he'd shown up here in the first place. He was still investigating her, still putting the case together, still trying to determine exactly what her father may have stolen and just how much she knew about it. He didn't have a search warrant yet, and now he'd tipped his hand.

Cursing his own stupidity, he said, "You'll get it soon enough. It's in the works."

"What the heck does that mean?" she demanded. Then her blue eyes flared as understanding hit her. "You don't have enough evidence. You think my father stole those documents, but you can't prove it. So you showed up here with your fake map just to see what kind of person I was. Or were you hoping you'd find a reason to arrest me?"

"I'm just doing my job," he said with a shrug. "If you've done nothing wrong, you've got nothing to worry about."

Fuming, she stepped around him to snatch open the front door to her shop. "I have nothing else to say to you. Get out. And next time you decide to check me out, you sure as hell better bring a search warrant."

When he hesitated, she added coldly, "The shop closed ten minutes ago. Don't make me call the police."

She would, Patrick thought with reluctant admiration. She had a hell of a lot of explaining to do about her shady business practices and the evidence that was piling up against her, and she was threatening to call the cops on him? She was something else.

"Save your call to the cops, and call a lawyer instead," he advised as he strode out. "You're going to need one."

When she slammed the door behind him, Patrick didn't even flinch. He wasn't impressed with her anger.

She was in the business of selling privately owned records of the past, and she had every right to sell anything she wanted that she'd bought from private citizens. But when she sold stolen documents from the National Archives, she was stealing the history of the United States.

And she wasn't going to get away with it, he promised himself. The problem was, even though he'd led her to believe differently, he didn't have a clue how many documents her father had really taken from the Archives. He'd tracked down those ten that had been sold on eBay, and knew for a fact that there weren't any more posted on the Internet, but that didn't mean anything. The more valuable items could have been sold to private buyers and would never see the light of day again. Without Mackenzie Sloan's cooperation— and records—his investigation was at a dead end.

He had to find a way to gain her trust, he decided, and the only way he could think of to do that was to appeal to her apparent love of history. If greed hadn't completely darkened her soul, she just might care enough about the loss of some of the documentation of the country's past to step up to the plate and help him. If that didn't work, then he'd appeal to her own self-preservation. She wouldn't like prison.

And he wouldn't like putting her there. There was nothing he liked more in a woman than intelligence, and she had plenty of that. When you added flashing blue eyes, a pretty face and plenty of spunk to the package, she was a hard woman to ignore.

Suddenly realizing where his thoughts had wandered, he swore softly as he reached his car. He didn't care how pretty she was; he wasn't interested in her as anything but a suspect. He had no use for a lying woman—he'd been there, done that—and had good reason to never trust any female other than his mother and aunts ever again. A smile from Mackenzie Sloan didn't change the fact that she was a suspect. And if his investigation proved that her father was guilty and her partner in crime, she was going to hate the day he ever walked in her shop. Because he would do everything he could to put her in jail.

Pacing restlessly, her stomach roiling with worry, Mackenzie snatched up the phone the second it rang. "Stacy! Thank God!"

"What's wrong?" she demanded. "I just got your message. Are you all right?"

Not sure if she wanted to cry or throw something, she said, "No, I'm not all right! You know that good-looking hunk you thought was so wonderful when you were here earlier? He's an agent with the National Archives, and he's investigating me."

"*What?* John and I will be there in ten minutes."

Eight minutes later, Stacy and her husband, John, rushed into the shop. Sinking into a chair at the reading table, Stacy rested her hand on her stomach and braced herself. "Don't sugarcoat it. Give me the worst. What are the Feds after and what did you say?"

"In a minute," Mackenzie said, frowning as she and John both stepped to her side. "Are you all right? I shouldn't have called you. I wasn't thinking."

"I'm your lawyer, silly," she scolded. "Of course you should have called me. And just because I'm pregnant, doesn't mean I can't work."

"You're supposed to be taking it easy," John reminded her. A tall, quiet man who absolutely adored his headstrong wife, he knew better than anyone that Stacy did what Stacy wanted to do. Still, he tried. "The doctor said—"

"He's an old woman, sweetheart," she said with a dismissive wave of her hand. "He worries too much. I'm fine."

Mackenzie exchanged a look with John, who only grinned and shrugged. Mackenzie couldn't be quite so blasé. Stacy was more than her best friend. She was the closest thing to family she had left. And from the moment she'd told her she was pregnant, Mackenzie had been worried to death about her.

And with good reason. She'd never been pregnant herself, but Mackenzie knew the risks. When she was twelve years old, her mother died in childbirth, and that tragedy still affected her sixteen years later. If something happened to Stacy…

"You still need to put your feet up," she said quickly. "Here, let me get you some tea."

Watching her flit around the shop, into the kitchen and back for hot tea and homemade cookies, then stoke the fire in the fireplace, Stacy finally said quietly, "It can't be that bad, Mac. Tell me."

Up until then, Mackenzie would have sworn that even though she was furious with Agent O'Reilly, she was in complete control of her emotions. Then tears came out of nowhere to sting her eyes. "I'm sorry," she choked, furiously wiping at the tears that spilled over her lashes. "I just can't believe this is happening. The Feds think Dad stole documents from the National Archives."

"*What?* You can't be serious."

"Oh, it gets better," she replied. "According to Agent O'Reilly, I knowingly sold the documents Dad stole on the Internet."

Her friend looked at her as if she'd lost her mind. "That's ridiculous! You've never done anything dishonest in your life, and neither did your dad. Agent O'Reilly's obviously made a mistake."

Mackenzie desperately wanted to believe her, but he'd seemed so sure. "He had a playbill I'd sold on eBay," she said, pacing restlessly. "It was from Ford's Theatre the night Lincoln was shot. He claims it was Lincoln's and belongs to the Archives."

"That seems like a difficult thing to prove unless it's got Lincoln's blood on it," John said, frowning. "Where did you get it?"

"From Dad. He told me he bought it from the descendant of a congressman who was in the audience that night."

"That's certainly possible," Stacy said. "Obviously, you believed him at the time. Why wouldn't you? The question is…do you still?"

Mackenzie had been asking herself that ever since Agent O'Reilly walked out the door. "I don't know," she admitted. "I don't want to believe Dad would do such a thing, but there's no other explanation. If that playbill really was stolen from the Archives, how did it end up in Dad's possession if he didn't steal it?"

"Maybe he bought it from the thief," Stacy suggested. "If that's the case, the story he told you was probably the same one the thief told him. He wasn't lying."

"Or he bought it from a legitimate owner," John pointed out. "Playbills would have been given to all the theatergoers at Ford's Theatre the night Lincoln was killed. How many people saved theirs? There's probably dozens of them in private collections."

"But wouldn't Agent O'Reilly know if it belonged to the Archives?" Stacy said, frowning.

"Not necessarily," Mackenzie replied and repeated what the agent had told her about how documents were inventoried at the Archives. "Just because a document doesn't have any stamps or file numbers doesn't mean it doesn't belong to the government."

"So he can't be sure that the playbill belongs to the Archives, either," John said. "If that's the case, why is he going after you?"

Mackenzie had been asking herself that ever since she'd kicked the irritating man out of her shop. "I don't know. The only thing I can think of is that he suspected Dad because he spent so much time at the Archives. Then when he checked eBay and saw that I had sold documents, he assumed they were ones stolen from the Archives."

"But he doesn't even know what's missing," Stacy pointed out indignantly. "It sounds like a witch hunt to me."

Mackenzie couldn't argue with that. "He's wasting his time," she assured her. "I know I didn't do anything wrong, and I'm going to prove it."

"It's not for you to prove your innocence. *He* has to prove your guilt, and that's going to be a tough thing to do since you've never done anything illegal in your life. Just don't talk to him again without your attorney present. Or show him your records! Okay?"

Mackenzie grinned. "Yes, ma'am."

"Smart-ass." She chuckled. Holding her hand out to her husband, she grinned. "Help me up, sweetheart."

He took her hand, but only to gently tug her to her feet so he could sweep her up into his arms. "John!" she laughed. "Put me down!"

"When we get to the car. You need to go home and put your feet up."

Laughing, she threw her arms around his neck and grinned at Mackenzie. "It looks like I have to go home now. If you hear from Agent O'Reilly again, call me immediately. Okay? This is serious, Mac. Don't deal with him by yourself."

"I won't," she promised, stepping over to give her and John a quick hug. "I'm sorry I had to drag you back here. You didn't even get to eat dinner, did you?"

"Don't worry about it." John chuckled. "We'll go through a drive-thru on the way home."

"John!"

"Say good-night, sweetheart, and I'll buy you an ice cream sundae, too."

Fighting a grin, she eyed him calculatingly. "Make it hot fudge, and you've got a deal."

"Hot fudge it is," he said promptly.

"Good night, sweetheart," she repeated obediently, winking at Mackenzie. "I'll call you tomorrow."

"Enjoy your sundae," she called after her, laughing, as John carried her outside. "Have one for me."

"I just might," she replied. "Don't worry. We'll get this straightened out tomorrow."

Mackenzie was still grinning as she locked the door behind them, but her smile quickly faded as her thoughts shifted back to Patrick O'Reilly. She wasn't a thief, and even though Stacy insisted that it was O'Reilly's responsibility to build a case against her, she didn't intend to leave anything to chance. The next time she saw the man, she'd be ready. She'd hit him with records on every item she'd ever sold.

Her blue eyes gleaming in anticipation, she strode into her office to start searching her records for receipts. Oh, yes, she was going to enjoy proving him wrong!

Chapter 3

The sun peeked over the horizon the following morning, ending the longest night of Mackenzie's life. Too worried to get more than three hours of sleep, she'd spent most of the night searching through her father's records for the playbill's receipt. It was like looking for fairy dust. There were loose papers literally everywhere—stuffed in the pages of books, on shelves, all over the shop's private upstairs apartment, even in the kitchen, for heaven's sake! And that was only the tip of the iceberg. The attic was overflowing.

Overwhelmed and so tired she could barely stand without swaying on her feet, she sank into a chair in front of the fireplace and fought the need to cry. She'd found plenty of receipts, but none that had anything to do with the playbill from Ford's Theatre. And that horrified her. What if Patrick O'Reilly was right about her father? Over the course of the last three months, she'd sold hundreds of historical letters and maps and rare books she'd inherited along with the shop. How many of them had been stolen?

Her blood chilling at the thought, she tried to convince herself she was overreacting. She was tired and obviously wasn't thinking straight. Just because she hadn't found any records didn't mean they didn't exist. She just hadn't come across them yet.

She would, she grimly promised herself. Even if she had to tear the shop apart. She just couldn't do it today. She had reserved a booth at a Civil War collectors' show that opened in Arlington in two hours, and she still had to pack her van and take a shower. Groaning at the thought, she pushed to her feet and hurriedly started filling a cardboard box with Civil War memorabilia for the show.

An hour and a half later, when she arrived at the collectors' show and started setting up her booth, she sent up a silent prayer of thanks for the wonders of a hot shower and a steaming cup of coffee. She was still tired—nothing short of some serious sleep was going to change that—but things didn't seem nearly as bleak as they had a few hours ago.

And there was nothing she loved more than historical collectors' shows. The history buffs who attended the shows lived and breathed American history and made no apologies for it. They always had a story to tell, a new collectible to show off, a research question they were hungry to have answered.

And then there were the rare books and private historical letters that the exhibitors sold at their individual booths. Invariably, someone always had a newly discovered map, letter or document for sale that no one else had even suspected existed, and it became the talk of the show. She couldn't wait to see what the buzz would be about today.

Setting up the last of her own exhibit, she checked to make sure everything was in its place, then turned, intending to take a quick tour of the room before the show opened to the public. She'd only taken two steps, however, when a pair of irritatingly familiar green eyes met hers across the room.

Agent Patrick O'Reilly.

Surprised, she frowned. What was he doing there?

Maybe he's following you to make sure you don't sell any more stolen documents.

The thought came out of nowhere, catching her off guard. Stunned, she told herself she was just being paranoid. He had better things to do than follow her around to shows and examine everything she sold. After all, he had no proof that she'd done anything unethical, let alone illegal. Was he here to harass her?

The very idea that he might do something to embarrass her in front of her customers and colleagues almost sent her storming across the small convention hall to confront him. But even as she considered telling him exactly what she thought of him, she knew that wouldn't be a wise move on her part. If the other exhibitors discovered that an agent from the National Archives was suspicious of her, the business her father had spent a lifetime building would be completely destroyed.

Swearing softly, she turned back to her booth. If Agent O'Reilly thought he was going to rattle her so easily, he could think again. She was made of sterner stuff than that.

Patrick usually worked memorabilia shows with Bill Rhoades, an investigative archivist with a photographic memory who could spot a counterfeit document without even lifting a magnifying glass to it. Bill, however, was home in bed, suffering from a nasty bout of food poisoning, so Patrick was on his own. Normally, he would have cancelled, but he'd wanted to see Mackenzie Sloan in action. If the lady thought she could sell stolen documents right under his nose, she could think again.

Setting up a card table, he laid out brochures that not only explained what the National Archives did, but also educated the public on how to spot a stolen document or one that should belong to the U.S. government. His real purpose here, however, was to check for stolen documents…which was why he planned to watch Mackenzie like a hawk. He didn't think she was brazen enough to sell a questionable item right in front of him, but the lady had already proven that she didn't lack for nerve when she had refused to cooperate unless he produced a search warrant. If she thought she could slide something past him when he wasn't looking, she just might try it.

The doors to the convention center opened then, and history lovers flooded inside. Patrick wasn't surprised by the size of the crowd. Collecting historical memorabilia was a popular pastime and very much a history buff's treasure hunt. Depending on their own particular interest, he'd seen people buy everything from Civil War ammunitions records to a stuffed buffalo head that supposedly had hung in Custer's office, though no one could really verify that for sure.

Grinning at the memory of the little old lady who had bought the buffalo, Patrick glanced over at Mackenzie…just in time to see her accept a credit card from a short, roly-poly elderly man who was looking at what appeared to be an old map. Clearly thrilled with his impending purchase, he grinned broadly as he waited for his receipt.

Swearing, Patrick headed straight for Mackenzie's booth. "Excuse me," he told the older man, "but would you mind if I took a look at that?"

"Of course he minds," Mackenzie retorted indignantly. "Go away."

Confused, the older man frowned at Patrick. "Who are you? Why do you want to look at my map?"

"I'm an agent with the National Archives, sir. I'm just checking for authenticity."

"Authenticity?" the man sputtered. "Are you saying it's fake?"

"No, of course not!" Mackenzie said quickly, scowling at Patrick. "Agent O'Reilly just meant—"

"There's been some items circulating in the D.C. area that should be in the National Archives," Patrick said easily.

The older man scowled fiercely. "What do you mean *should be?* Are they stolen?"

"Not necessarily," Mackenzie answered before

Patrick could reply. "Documents fall into private hands all the time. That doesn't mean they're stolen."

"That's right," Patrick agreed. "With time, some documents become less important and the government releases them into the public domain. And sometimes they don't, and even dealers like Ms. Sloan don't realize that they are stolen. We've had a lot of calls about it, so we've been checking out the shows, seeing if we can discover what's going on. So if you don't mind…"

He lifted a dark brow at the other man, silently asking permission to examine the map. Without a word, he handed it to Patrick.

Beside him, Patrick could practically feel Mackenzie seething. She didn't, however, say a word as he unrolled the map.

It was a hand-drawn, colorful map that depicted the Colonies before the Revolutionary War broke out, complete with cities, rivers, forests and ports. It was an important map and beautifully drawn, the kind of thing that a history buff would love to have hanging over his mantel. There were, however, no forts on the map, no military encampments or anything that connected it to the upcoming war. And while it was historical, it wasn't something that appeared to have ever belonged in the Archives.

Whether it was stolen from another museum or library, however, was another matter. There was nothing the least bit suspicious about it, though, so Patrick had no choice but to believe that Mackenzie had acquired it legitimately.

She would, no doubt, gloat over that, but he'd never been afraid to err on the side of caution. Especially, he thought, when all the evidence he'd been able to collect on Mackenzie so far pointed to the fact that when it came to her business, she was not a woman to be trusted.

Handing the map back to its new owner, he said, "Congratulations, sir. You bought a great map."

"You're sure it's not stolen?"

"As sure as I can be," Patrick replied. "Take it home and enjoy it."

He didn't have to tell him twice. Pleased, the older man hugged his new treasure and moved on to the next booth.

He was hardly out of earshot when Mackenzie hissed, "What do you think you're doing? This is harassment!"

Far from concerned, he only grinned. "Are you kidding? You think I'm harassing you because I checked what you're selling? That's my job. It's nothing personal."

"So why aren't you checking anyone else's documents?" she demanded. "Why are you just watching me?"

"As far as I know, no one else here is selling stolen documents on the Internet. If you know someone else who is, point them out and I'll be happy to check them out."

Horrified that he was making no effort to keep his voice down, she caught the curious glances of nearby vendors and wanted to sink right through the floor. Heat spilling into her cheeks, she grabbed him by the arm and hauled him into the narrow hallway that led to the restrooms.

"You've got to stop this!" she snapped in a low voice that didn't carry past the hallway. "Do you hear me? If you don't back off, I'm calling the police!"

Far from impressed, he lifted a mocking brow at her. "Are you sure you want to do that? Right now, you just have to deal with me, and I'm easy. You bring in the local cops and you could have all kinds of headaches. But if you really want to talk to someone, use my phone. The reception is probably better on mine. Go ahead. I've got unlimited minutes."

More frustrated than she'd ever been in her life, Mackenzie gave serious thought to telling him exactly what she thought of him, and she didn't care who heard her. And that stunned her. She was usually easygoing and rarely lost her temper. But there was something about Patrick O'Reilly that drove her crazy.

"You know something, you're a very irritating man," she said, scowling at him as a mocking smile curled the corners of his mouth. "You think you have me right where you want me, don't you?"

Amused, he said, "Don't I?"

"No," she retorted. "For your information, you're in danger of making a complete fool of yourself."

His mouth twitched into a smile. "Really? And that concerns you?"

"Not at all," she said dryly. "If you want to waste your time trying to prove I'm a thief while the real thief gets away with stealing thousands of dollars' worth of historical documents from the American people, have at it. It's your career."

"It's yours, too," he pointed out. "Of course, maybe you don't care about your reputation. Maybe you just want to unload everything, get out from under the business and go back to California."

Surprised, she blinked. "How do you know I lived in California?"

"I checked you out, of course," he retorted, grinning.

"I know everything about you, right down to that C you made in biology your second year of college at Duke and the name of your first boyfriend."

"Oh, really?"

"He really was a nerd, Mackenzie. What were you thinking?"

Steaming, Mackenzie couldn't miss the amusement dancing in his eyes. Oh, he was enjoying this. And as much as she didn't want to admit it, he was incredibly charming. All too easily, she could imagine what he was like when he pursued a woman: fun, teasing, wickedly mischievous. The kind of man, she silently acknowledged, that she'd always had a weakness for.

The thought came out of nowhere to steal the breath right out of her lungs. Had she lost her mind? He was right. What was she thinking?

"So now that I know just about everything there is to know about you, are you going to trust me and let me look at your files or not?"

Thankful that he'd brought the subject back to the matter at hand, she looked at him sharply. *Trust.* It was such an easy word. And even though he'd checked her out, she seriously doubted that he had a clue just how difficult it was for her to trust anyone.

It was, she silently acknowledged, something she'd struggled with for a long, long time…ever since her mother died and she discovered that there were no guarantees in life. If you couldn't count on the people you loved to always be there for you, how could you count on strangers?

And what, after all, did she know about Patrick

O'Reilly? she reminded herself. She didn't know if he was a man of his word or not, if he was the kind to trick a "suspect" into confiding in him so he could then use that confidence to haul the poor trusting idiot off to jail. Could she really take a chance and trust him when she didn't know for sure if her father had stolen documents from the Archives? What kind of charges could she be setting herself up for if some of the documents she'd sold really had belonged to the Archives?

"Look," he said when she hesitated, "we got off to a bad start. Okay? I'm not trying to destroy your business or your father's reputation. I'm just trying to get to the truth. If your father didn't steal those documents, then he bought them from whoever did and you sold them. I need to know who that person is, and you can help me. Somewhere in your father's papers, there's bound to be a record of who he bought these things from. I just need this jackass's name, but you're protecting him by refusing to let me look at your father's records."

Surprised, Mackenzie hadn't thought of it that way. "I'm not protecting anyone," she retorted, stung.

"Of course you are. And frankly, I don't understand why. You're so concerned about protecting your father's reputation, but you're protecting the one person who could have destroyed it. Is that what you really want?"

"No, of course not!"

"Then talk to me!"

"My lawyer told me not to."

He frowned. "If you haven't done anything wrong, what do you need a lawyer for?" Before she could even begin to answer, understanding dawned. "This is about your father."

"He was an honorable man," she said huskily. "He would have never knowingly bought anything stolen."

"So what are you saying? You're not responsible for what's in his shop?"

"Yes."

"Did I imply that you were?"

When she blinked in surprise, Patrick was stunned. Did she really think she was going to be hanged for the sins of her father? Okay, so he'd come down hard on her. He took his job seriously, and when he'd first started investigating her, she and her father had looked guilty as hell. But there were some things he couldn't deny. Up until his death, Michael Sloan had had an impeccable reputation. What if he hadn't stolen those documents? What if his sin was that of being too trusting? It was that thought that nagged at Patrick and refused to be ignored.

"Whatever your father may or may not have done has nothing to do with you. Unless," he added, "you continue to sell things you know were probably stolen. You're taking a huge risk, Mackenzie. Are you sure you want to do that?"

When her gaze shifted to her unattended booth, where the items she'd brought to sell were clearly displayed, he knew the second she made up her mind to cooperate. She lifted her chin, squared her shoulders, and met his gaze dead on.

"I'm not trying to be difficult. I have nothing to hide. If my lawyer says it's okay, you're welcome to check my father's records whenever you like."

Pleased, he said, "Good. Then I'll follow you back to your shop after the show. I'd like to get started on this as soon as possible."

A steady influx of history buffs streamed into the memorabilia show over the course of the day. It was one of the best shows Mackenzie had been to since she'd taken over the business. But as she packed up at the end of the day and headed home, her attention was on the man who followed her at a safe distance in his black SUV.

After she'd agreed to give him access to her father's business records, Patrick's attitude had completely changed. He'd gone back to his own table, then spent the rest of the afternoon greeting history buffs and handing out literature. She'd watched him laugh and joke with people and turn serious over the subject he was there to discuss—the theft and sale of archival documents and what to watch for.

To her dismay, he'd completely distracted her from her own sales.

"You're losing it, Mac," she warned herself aloud as she drove through the familiar streets of Washington. "The man is a federal agent who went after you like a pit bull. His interest in you is strictly business."

Later, she knew, he would probably haunt the sleep she so desperately needed, but she couldn't worry about him now. She had better things to do. Like finding a parking place.

At any other time, that could have been an exercise in frustration, but as she slowly made her way up and down the streets within walking distance of her shop, she had to smile. She loved D.C. during the holidays. Christmas might be nearly a month away—the Capitol and National Christmas trees hadn't even been lit yet—but the shops and cafés in her neighborhood were already decked out for the season and glistening with twinkling lights. Not surprisingly, business was brisk.

Which was why, she thought with a rueful smile, she didn't find a parking spot on the first swipe down her street. She circled the block four times before she spied a Mini Cooper pulling out of a tiny space in front of the Chinese grocery down the street from her shop. Thankfully, her PT Cruiser didn't take up a lot of room, and she whipped into the space, lightning-quick, before anyone else could take it. It wasn't until she stepped out of her car and turned to see where Patrick was that she realized she had lost him while she was hunting for a parking space.

He knew where the shop was, she reminded herself as twilight slipped into darkness and the streetlights popped on. He'd find her. In the meantime, she had to unload her car. Pulling two boxes from the backseat, she headed for her shop.

The building was over a hundred and fifty years old, and during its long history, it had been everything from a photography studio to an Indian restaurant to a funeral parlor. In its first incarnation, however, it had been a tavern, and it still retained its original bow window, fireplace and rich wainscoting. Her father had taken one look at it and known it was just what he was looking for. Laid out like a house, with a bedroom upstairs and the kitchen and common rooms downstairs, it was the perfect setup for a shop owner. He'd bought it on the spot six months after Mackenzie's mother died, and he and Mackenzie had moved in immediately. Here she'd worked through her grief and grown up in the security of her father's love. She couldn't imagine living or working anywhere else.

Patrick came around the corner then and hurried forward to help her with her load as she reached the front door of her shop. "Here…let me help you with that. You should have waited for me."

"Thanks." She sighed in relief. "I didn't know where you had gone. Where'd you park?"

"Around the corner," he began, only to swear softly when she started to slip her key in the lock and the door silently glided open. Glancing at her sharply in the darkness, he growled, "Did you lock the door when you left?"

She frowned. "I always lock it when I leave the shop, even if it's just to drop a letter in the mailbox on the corner."

"You're sure?"

"Of course. I set the alarm, too." Her gaze drifting back to the open door, she glanced back up at him in confusion. "I don't understand. Why didn't the alarm go off? The door's open. It should have gone off."

His face carved in grim lines, Patrick reached for his phone. "I don't know," he retorted. "But I'm going to find out."

"Who are you calling?"

"The cops. Breaking and entering is out of my jurisdiction."

* * *

Less than fifteen minutes later, a patrol car arrived and braked to a stop right in the middle of the narrow street. Standing at Mackenzie's side, Patrick took one look at the officer who stepped out of the car and grinned. "What the devil are you doing here? I thought you had the day off."

"I switched shifts with Larry Lopez. What's going on? Did you make the call?"

Patrick nodded and explained about the unlocked door of the bookstore. "This is Mackenzie Sloan—she owns the store. Mackenzie, this is my brother, Devin."

"Oh, my God. There are two of you in law enforcement?"

Grinning, Devin shook the hand she held out to him. "Actually, there's three of us," he admitted. "Logan's with the FBI."

"It's in the blood," Patrick explained. "Our father was a cop, too."

"So what are you doing here?" Devin asked him, frowning.

Quickly giving him a rundown about the stolen items that had somehow ended up in Mackenzie's father's possession, he added, "I followed Mackenzie home from a show in Arlington to look at her father's records. That's when we found the door open."

"And it was locked when you left?" Devin asked Mackenzie as he jotted down notes.

"There's not a doubt in my mind I locked it," she said firmly. "The lock on the door sticks sometimes, so I always check it twice. It was definitely locked."

"And the alarm? Is there a possibility you may have forgotten to activate it?"

"No. I was on the phone to my friend Stacy, and distinctly remember setting the alarm on my way out."

"And no one else has a key or the alarm code?" Devin asked. "A neighbor? An old boyfriend?"

She shook her head. "No, no one. I've been meaning to change the code since my father died and give the new code and a key to Stacy, but I just haven't had time."

"Then your father must have given it to someone," Patrick said.

Startled, Mackenzie paled. "You think one of his friends would have broke into the shop?"

"It's possible," he said. "Unless the alarm malfunctioned, whoever left the door open had to have the code. If you didn't give it to anyone, then your father had to."

"We won't know the truth until we check it out," Devin said. "C'mon. Let's go." Quietly ordering Mackenzie to stay outside until they scoured the building, he stepped around Mackenzie and carefully, soundlessly pushed open the door. Seconds later, he and Patrick slipped inside.

Chapter 4

Not quite sure what to expect when she was finally allowed inside, Mackenzie felt her stomach knot with nerves as she showed the two men where the alarm system was, then left them to inspect it as she looked around the shop. In every room, there was a fortune in vintage maps and historical documents, not to mention first edition and rare books. If whoever let themselves in really knew her father, then they would, in all likelihood, know where the more valuable items were.

However, everything looked just as it had when she'd left. For the most part, she knew where things were, though she couldn't have said if a particular book or map was missing unless it was something that was usually displayed in plain sight. A quick glance showed her that the more visible items hadn't been touched.

Joining her a few minutes later as she surveyed the shelves that held a wide assortment of rare books, the two men waited patiently while she inspected one room after another. "Well?" Patrick said finally. "Does it look like anything's missing?"

"Not that I can tell," she said, "but I won't know for sure until I spend some serious time going through everything." Glancing at Devin's grim expression, she braced herself for the verdict on the alarm system. "Someone has a key, don't they?"

He nodded. "Unless you're mistaken about setting the alarm and locking the door, that's the only explanation."

Chilled at the thought of someone walking through the shop, the apartment, her bedroom, she shivered. "I've got to get the locks changed."

"You can call a locksmith and have them changed tonight," Patrick assured her. "I'll help you. But first, whoever let himself in here didn't do it just to see if he could get away with it. He was after something, and odds are, he found it."

"But it doesn't look like he took anything," she said, frowning as she once again looked around the shop. "Nothing's been touched."

"Nothing *appears* to have been touched," Devin corrected her. "You live and work here, and when you're in a place all the time, it's easy to overlook your surroundings. Take your time and walk through the place again. This time, look at little things—a book in a different place than you remembered, a drawer not quite closed, something on the shelves filed wrong. Whoever let himself into your shop had to touch *something*. We just have to find out what it was."

He made it sound so simple. But as Mackenzie slowly inspected the public area of the shop again, she couldn't find so much as a smidgen of dust that had been disturbed. Nothing, not even a piece of paper, let alone a document or a book, was out of place.

Frustrated, she headed upstairs with the two men following behind her. She was missing something. She could feel it in her bones. But as she went through her bedroom, then the guest room and her father's office, which she hadn't had the heart to move downstairs where it would have been more convenient, everything was right where she'd left it.

Except a pile of old receipts on her father's desk.

At first she didn't notice them. She stood in the middle of the office and looked around and saw nothing out of the ordinary. Then, just as she started to turn and walk out of the room, she saw them. They hadn't been there the night before.

"What?" Patrick demanded, immediately noting her change in expression. Following her gaze, he frowned. "What do you see?"

"The receipts on the corner of the desk," she said. "I was going through them last night, but I put them back in the filing cabinet when I finished with them."

"Going through them?" Devin asked. "For what?"

"She was looking for proof that her old man really bought a playbill that was stolen from the Archives," Patrick answered for her. "I take it you didn't find it?" he asked her.

Grimacing, she said, "I didn't find anything that mentioned a playbill or even hinted at anything to do with Lincoln or Ford's Theatre. Unless it was written in code, it wasn't there."

"Maybe whoever let himself in was looking for a receipt to something a hell of a lot more valuable than a playbill," Devin pointed out.

"And we don't have a clue what that might be," Patrick said in disgust. "Damn! Unless he was stupid enough to leave fingerprints, we're back to square one."

"Only one way to find out." Devin reached for his phone. "I'm calling the evidence team."

From everything that Patrick had seen of Mackenzie Sloan, she was a strong woman who wasn't afraid of anything, especially a federal agent intent on investigating her business. But an hour and a half later as the evidence team left and the locksmith finished changing the locks, there was no question that the lady was shaken. She stood pale and drawn in front of the cold fireplace, her arms wrapped around herself, her eyes dark and shadowy with fear.

Watching her, Patrick couldn't blame her for being more than a little uneasy. She had good reason to be afraid.

Whoever had slipped into the shop was, in Patrick's opinion, one of the worst kinds of criminal. The intruder was most likely an acquaintance of the family, someone who was liked and trusted, someone who may have attended her father's funeral, or offered to help her with the shop any time she felt overwhelmed. Someone who, Patrick could just imagine, had looked Mackenzie right in the eye any number of times over the course of the past three months and tried to sell her more stolen documents.

Patrick swore silently at the thought. How many of her father's friends did she have dealings with? Did she realize that whoever had the key and code could come into her shop and her apartment any damn time he pleased? Had he slipped in while she slept at night? Had he been watching her?

The sudden anger surprised him. What the hell was he doing? he wondered, stiffening. There was nothing to indicate that the intruder was some kind of pervert or that he had any plans to hurt Mackenzie. He was just a thief trying to cover his tracks, and the odds were he hadn't let himself in when Mackenzie was home. He didn't have to. In all likelihood, he knew her well enough to know her routine and that she spent many of her Saturdays at memorabilia shows. All he had to do was ask her when the next show was, then let himself into the shop after she left.

Every instinct Patrick had told him that whoever the thief was, he wouldn't hurt Mackenzie. He could have already done that if that was his intention. The bastard probably even had some affection for her. She was safe.

So why was he still here? he wondered, irritated with himself. Why hadn't he left when Devin and the evidence team had? He had the names and phone numbers of all her father's friends—there was nothing more he needed from her. She'd changed the locks and the alarm code— she couldn't have been any more secure in Fort Knox. She didn't need him to worry about her, let alone babysit her.

He knew that, accepted it. Yet instead of telling her

good-night, he heard himself say, "Are you going to be all right here by yourself?"

Wherever she was in her thoughts, it was a deep, dark place. He had to ask her twice before she heard him. Dragging her gaze from the fire, she turned to face him. "I'm fine," she said stiffly. "I was just thinking."

"That's not what I asked you. Will you be scared here by yourself?"

"I have new locks—"

"Answer the question, Mackenzie."

She stiffened at that, her blue eyes flashing fire. "What do you want to hear? That I'm frightened? That I won't be able to sleep tonight? That the thought of a friend of my father's slipping in here like a thief in the night infuriates me and terrifies me at one and the same time?"

"Mackenzie—"

"Who do you think it is? Uncle Steve? Or maybe Papa Joe? And then there's Stan the man. He was Dad's roommate in college and best man at his wedding to my mother. He's like family. If Dad gave a key to anyone other than me, it would be Stan. Do you think he went through the cash drawer? Or through Dad's private collection of early American maps? Maybe he helped himself to a few—if he sold those to a private collector, he wouldn't have to work the rest of his life. Maybe I'll call and ask him—"

Patrick had never seen a woman closer to a meltdown, and his heart broke for her. He shouldn't have pushed her for an answer. She'd been through an emotional hailstorm, and she had every right to be on the edge.

"You don't have to do that," he assured her. "I'll question Stan in the morning."

"I don't need your permission to call my godfather," she retorted. "I can talk to him whenever I want. Do you hear me? I've known him all my life and he would never do anything to hurt me."

"I didn't say that he would," he said patiently. "I'm not the bad guy here, sweetheart. Don't shoot. I'm just trying to help."

Her eyes narrowed dangerously. "Don't call me sweetheart."

Patrick liked to think he was a smart man. And a smart man didn't argue with a woman who gave him *that* look...not if he wanted to keep his hair.

"Yes, ma'am. Whatever you say, ma'am."

"Don't call me ma'am, either," she snapped. "I'm not your grandmother."

"No, ma'am," he said dryly. "You're certainly not."

He was just trying to pacify her. Instead, he'd pushed her over the edge.

Advancing on him with fire in her eyes, she grabbed him by the arm to pull him to the door. "Out!" she ordered, tugging at him. "Get out!"

He didn't budge. Instead, he covered her hand with his where it rested on his arm. "Mackenzie, it's okay. You're safe. I know you're scared—"

"I am not!"

"Okay, so you're not. You still don't need to be alone right now. You're obviously upset—"

"I'm fine!"

But even as she tried to convince him and herself,

tears streamed down her face. She tried to stop them, to hide them from him, but a sob rose in her throat, and just that quickly, she lost the battle. Bowing her head, she buried her face in her hands and cried.

Patrick swallowed a groan. He liked to think that he was capable of handling whatever life threw at him, but a woman's tears had always destroyed him. Maybe it was because his mother had tried so hard to be strong for him and his brothers after their father was killed in the line of duty, but there'd been times when fear had overcome her and she'd cried. He could still remember how helpless he'd felt at the time. And he'd learned then that when a woman was reduced to tears, there was nothing a man could do but hold her and assure her everything was going to be all right.

Every instinct warned him that Mackenzie Sloan was the last woman he should try to console. From the moment he'd first laid eyes on her, there was something about her that he found hard to ignore. He didn't know if it was the spark of defiance in her eyes, the jut of her chin when she dared him to return with a search warrant or the quick smile and laugh that she shared with her customers at the memorabilia show. Whatever it was, he knew he needed to keep her at a distance.

That, however, was impossible when the sound of her sobs pulled at him in a way he hadn't expected. Before he could stop himself, he found himself pulling her into her arms. "Shh," he murmured. "It's going to be okay. Don't cry."

He might as well have asked the wind not to blow.

Pressing her face against his chest, she cried, "I—I c-can't help it."

"I know," he said gruffly. "You've been through a rough time and you're handling it all by yourself. Anybody would break."

"I'm sorry." She sniffed. "I'm not supposed to do this."

"Do what?"

"Cry all over the man who wants to arrest me. It's terrible etiquette."

Patrick just barely bit back a groan. He'd never met a woman who could laugh at herself at the same time she was having a meltdown. Did she know how appealing that was? How was he supposed to deal with that? How was he supposed to deal with *her?*

"I don't want to arrest you," he said gruffly. "I'm just trying to do my job."

"But you think I deliberately sold stolen documents."

"That's what I thought when you refused to let me look at your records," he said when she pulled back to look up at him with eyes red from crying. "But since whoever was in here appears to have helped themselves to the only evidence you had that proved your father bought the stolen documents, there's obviously someone else involved. Unless you paid someone to break in to the shop—"

"What? No! I would have never thought to do such a thing."

"Then it's looking more and more like your father— and you—were the real victims here. So stop crying, okay? Whoever broke in here tonight did you a favor."

The tears that had stopped suddenly welled in her

eyes again. "I'm sorry," she choked, swiping at her damp cheeks. "I guess I didn't realize how all this was affecting me. Tonight was just the straw that broke the camel's back."

"It sounds like it's been a long time coming," he told her, and pulled a clean handkerchief from his pocket. "No wonder you almost took my head off. And all I was trying to do was help you."

"Yeah, right." She chuckled. "You were harassing me and you know it. I was just defending—"

Her gaze locked with his, Mackenzie never saw him lift his hand, never realized his intentions until he gently wiped her damp cheek with his handkerchief. Suddenly, he was whisper-close, and there didn't seem to be any oxygen left in the shop. For the life of her, she couldn't remember how to breathe.

"Don't."

She'd meant to sound firm and cool, but her voice was anything but. Horrified, she ordered herself to move, to put some space between them, to thank him for his help and send him on his way. Her feet, however, refused to move. And it was all Patrick's fault. If he would just stop touching her...

Unable to take her eyes from him, she reached blindly for his hand. "I'm fine," she said huskily. "You have to stop."

But instead of pushing his hand away, she clung to it like a lifeline.

The feel of her fingers wrapped around his caught Patrick off guard. This was crazy. Just that morning, she'd been a suspect, and now he all he could think about was the softness of her skin, her mouth…and kissing her.

He should have stepped back right then and there, wished her good-night and made sure he never got that close to the lady again. Instead, he tightened his hand around hers and pulled her back into his arms. She only had time to gasp softly before his mouth covered hers.

Sweet. Hot. Decadent. She had the kind of mouth a man could lose himself in. His head whirling, he just wanted to wrap his arms tighter around her and sink into her. Just for a minute. What would it hurt?

Even as the question bounced around in his head, he remembered all too clearly what it was like to be taken in by a woman. Carla, his ex, had been as soft and kissable as Mackenzie Sloan—and the biggest liar he'd ever met in his life. When she'd gotten pregnant, he'd done the right thing and married her. Then when their son was three years old, she'd told him she wanted a divorce…and oh, by the way, the son he adored wasn't really his.

The pain of that brought him back to his senses as nothing else could. He wasn't ever again setting himself up for that kind of heartache. Abruptly releasing Mackenzie, he stepped back.

Swallowing a curse, he growled, "Are you going to be all right here by yourself?"

Her heart thundering, Mackenzie struggled to steady her legs under her and managed to take a step back. *All right?* she thought, shaken. Was he serious? Of course she wasn't all right! He'd just turned her world upside down, and she didn't know if she wanted to cry or step back into his arms. What had he done to her?

"I'm sure I'll be fine," she said huskily, and tried to believe it. "I've got new locks and a new alarm code. There's nothing to be scared of."

Frowning, he studied her with sharp green eyes that seemed to see to her very soul. "No, there's not," he agreed. "Whoever broke in here tonight wasn't your average two-bit street thug who steals to support his drug habit. And his profile probably matches every one of your dad's friends—smart, educated, history lover."

"He's not much of a history lover if he's stealing it," she snapped.

"True, but he doesn't see it that way. If he's true to type, he's probably fallen on hard times and needs money. And as far as he's concerned, federal documents belong to the American public. He's an American. In his mind, he's just taking what's his."

"That's ridiculous!"

"I agree, but that's what criminals do—find a way to justify their actions. And when they're caught, they usually give up without a fight and spill their guts. You don't have to be afraid of this man, Mackenzie. He's not going to hurt you."

There was no doubting his sincerity, and he had no idea how that relieved her mind. "I'm going to hold you to that," she warned, "so you'd better be right."

"You got it," he retorted, grinning, and pulled out a business card. "That's my cell phone number," he told her as he gave her his card. "If you have any trouble—I don't care if the wind blows wrong and rattles the windows and you think someone's trying to break in—call me. It doesn't matter what time it is, I'll make sure you're safe. Okay?"

Another man might have said the same just to make her feel better and not meant a word of it, but something told her that Patrick was dead serious. And he had no idea how that touched her. She hadn't realized until now just how alone and vulnerable she'd felt since her father died and she had returned to D.C.

"Thank you," she said huskily. "I'm sure I'll be fine. If the windows start rattling, though…"

"I'll be here," he finished for her, grinning. "And so will the rest of my brothers if you need us."

"Yeah, right." She laughed. "I really think you would, but the FBI and MPDC? For a creaking floorboard in the middle of the night? They've got better things to do."

"Than save a damsel in distress? I don't think so."

The clock on the mantel struck nine, reminding them both that he'd been there for hours. "I've taken up enough of your time," she said, sobering. "Thank you for your help. I'm sorry about the receipts."

"Don't beat yourself up over it," he cut in. "How could you have anticipated that someone would break in just to steal receipts? *I* didn't anticipate it!"

"Obviously, he figured out that the thefts had been discovered," she said. "But how?"

He shrugged. "It's hard to say. He could have been at the show today and saw the two of us talking and put two and two together. Or he saw the documents you posted on eBay and realized it was only a matter time before the thefts were discovered and he had to move fast to protect himself. Hopefully, the fingerprints the evidence team collected tonight will provide some answers. Right now, that seems to be the only hope we have."

"You'll keep me posted?"

"Of course. Try not to worry about it, okay? I'll be in touch."

And with no more warning than that, he wished her good-night and left.

Later, Mackenzie couldn't have said how long she stood there after she locked the door behind him, listening to the beating of her own heart, remembering a kiss that never should have happened. It was just a kiss, she told herself…and tried with all her heart to believe it. But she'd had her share of "just kisses," and there'd been nothing the least bit ordinary about *that* kiss. It was…the lighting of the Eiffel Tower on New Year's Eve, seeing Rome for the first time, a thousand shooting stars in the night sky.

"And you've been reading too many romance novels," she muttered as she turned off the downstairs lights and headed upstairs. "Get real."

But later, as she crawled into bed and closed her eyes, she only had to think of Patrick and *that kiss* to see the Eiffel Tower on New Year's Eve.

She was in big, big trouble.

Chapter 5

There were, Patrick decided, some things a man would be wiser to forget, and kissing Mackenzie Sloan was one of them. Unfortunately, he was having a difficult time doing that, and it was all her fault. Every time he let his guard down, she slipped uninvited into his thoughts, teasing him, haunting him, seducing him. It had been well over a week since he'd lost all reason and pulled her into his arms for a kiss that never should have happened, and he could still taste her on his tongue.

And it was driving him crazy! It was just a kiss, he tried to tell himself for the thousandth time. It was no big deal. So why couldn't he forget it? Why couldn't he forget *her?* He'd kissed his share of pretty women before.

He'd never, however, mooned over one for a week afterwards. Except for Carla.

His jaw clenched just at the thought of his ex-wife. When he'd fallen in love with her and married her, he'd truly thought the two of them had found the kind of love his parents had, the kind that lasted a lifetime. What he'd loved, however, had been nothing but a dream, a fantasy. She hadn't shown him who she really was until she'd taken his son away from him forever.

Because of her, he didn't know if he'd ever be able to trust a woman again. So why had he given Mackenzie permission to haunt his every waking moment? He'd kept his distance—hers wasn't the only case he was investigating. Okay, so he'd called her three times. He'd kept the conversation short and just discussed the case. It hadn't mattered. He still found himself looking for her in the faces of other women and driving past her shop whenever he was in her part of town. What the hell was he doing? What was it about her he couldn't forget?

He had to stop thinking about her, he thought as he headed to his mother's for dinner. His only connection to Mackenzie was the stolen documents. Once they were found, he would have no other contact with her. Unfortunately, he'd done nothing but run into one brick wall after another. He'd questioned everyone on the list of friends Mackenzie had given him, and not one of them admitted to having a key to the shop. And they all had alibis for the night the shop was broken into. At a dead end, his lone hope was that Devin would come back with some idents of the fingerprints the evidence team had found at the shop.

"Hey, there you are," his mother said as he strode into the kitchen. Pleased, she turned from the stove to give him a quick hug. "Get the salad out of the fridge, sweetie, while I get the lasagna. Did you have a rough day? Devin said the two of you are working on a case together."

Patrick just barely swallowed a groan. He did *not* want to talk about the case! That would only lead to a discussion about Mackenzie, and he didn't want to go there with his mother. He could just hear her now. Who was this woman, Mackenzie? Was she pretty? Was she married? Did he like her—

His mother's words suddenly registered, and he looked at her sharply as she carried the bubbling lasagna to the kitchen table. "What did Devin tell you?"

"Oh, just that you discovered some stolen items on eBay," Kate O'Reilly said as he pulled out a chair at the kitchen table and settled across from her. "He said there was a woman involved."

He was, Patrick decided, going to shoot his brother. He should have known he'd set him up this way. There was nothing Devin enjoyed more than setting him up. Before Patrick could deny there was anything going on between Mackenzie and himself, however, his mother bowed her head for grace.

Another man might have been relieved—maybe she'd forget—but he knew his mother too well. There was nothing she wanted more than for all three of her sons to find women to love and spend the rest of their lives with. And if they couldn't find someone on their own, then she was happy to assist them.

Which was why, he thought with a reluctant grin, he wasn't surprised when she lifted her head at the end of the prayer and looked up at him with a sweet, inquiring smile. "So…Devin says this Mackenzie woman is very pretty."

"Mom—"

"Don't *Mom* me. You know I just want you to be happy. So…have you asked her out yet? You could invite her to the New Year's Eve party. I'd love to meet her."

His mother's annual New Year's Eve party was something family and friends looked forward to every year, and Patrick—and his brothers—never missed it. Patrick had, however, learned a long time ago not to bring a date. His mother always jumped to the conclusion that he'd found the woman of his dreams, and he wasn't going there again!

"She was a suspect, Mom. Nothing more."

"*Was?* So she's not anymore?"

Patrick swallowed a groan. He should have known she'd jump on that one word. "She doesn't appear to be a suspect anymore, but it doesn't matter. I'm not looking for a date or a lover or anything else. I'm not going there, and you know why."

Kate O'Reilly didn't pretend to misunderstand. Tears immediately misted her eyes. "Oh, honey, I'm sorry! I can only imagine what all this has been like for you. Have you seen Tommy?"

"No," he said flatly. "I don't ever expect to see him again."

"Don't say that!"

"It's true, Mom. The judge ruled I had no rights since I'm not really his father, and that's all Carla needed to cut me out of his life."

"But she knows how much Tommy loves you," she

argued. "You're the only father he's ever known. And it's Christmas! Surely just this once, she'll be reasonable and think of Tommy."

Patrick desperately wanted to believe her, but he'd called Carla dozens of times after the divorce and tried to work out some kind of visitation with her. He'd refused to give up until she threatened to file harassment charges against him.

"I'm not counting on that," he said huskily. "You know how Carla is, Mom. Once she makes a decision, she doesn't budge."

He could tell she wanted to argue, but they both knew he was right. Blinking back tears, she reached across the table to squeeze his hand. "Just try not to give up hope. Things will get better, even though it might not seem that way right now."

She'd always been one of those people who saw the glass as half-full, which was incredible, considering the fact that she'd been widowed at the age of thirty-five and left with three sons to raise alone. Patrick wasn't nearly as optimistic, especially when it came to his son. Not after months of hitting his head against a wall and getting nowhere. As much as it killed him to admit it, he had to accept the fact that there were some things he couldn't change, and the loss of his son was one of them.

He didn't, however, have the heart to say that to his mother. She was just trying to help. "I know, Mom. I'm trying to be positive."

"You might feel better if you went out more—"

"Mom—"

"And met some nice women."

She was nothing if not persistent. Laughing, he gave in gracefully. "I'll see what I can do. Okay? Does that make you happy?"

She grinned, pleased. "Absolutely. Did I tell you Mary Walker's niece just moved to D.C.? I've seen her picture. She's beautiful…"

At four in the morning, the streets of Capitol Hill were dark and deserted. There was no moon, and the only sound was the whispered rustle of fallen leaves being pushed along by a cold breeze. Then, somewhere in the distance, the sound of a siren ripped through the night as an ambulance raced through the empty streets toward George Washington University Hospital.

The residents of Capitol Hill, however, slept on, undisturbed. And in the dark shadows that shrouded the streets, no one saw the figure that soundlessly moved from shadow to shadow, blending in with the night.

When a dog suddenly barked, the night itself seemed to hold its breath. The dark figure froze, and for a long, tense moment, nothing seemed to move. Then, as quickly as the dog broke into a startled bark, he abruptly hushed. Once again, silence permeated the night.

Still, the figure dressed all in black stood rooted to the ground, waiting another ten long minutes before daring to move. And even then, it was hardly discernible as it clung to the deepest shadows of the night and traveled down the street.

Halfway down the block, Sloan Antiquarian Books and Maps was almost invisible in the night but for the lighted display window that was decorated for Christmas. Flanked on both sides by two evergreen bushes, the front door was locked tight, and there wasn't a security camera in sight.

Soundlessly, the figure in black was swallowed whole by the darkness that enveloped the front door. On the empty street, there were no witnesses as a key was slipped into the lock…and no one to hear the soft curse when the key wouldn't turn. With more muttered curses, the thief in the night tried to turn the key again and pushed on the door with a shoulder.

A split second later, the security alarm screamed like a banshee.

Sound asleep, Mackenzie came awake with a start. What…? Then she heard it. The alarm.

Just that quickly, she was terrified. Her heart thundering, she threw off the covers and reached for the phone in the dark. Before she could even punch in 911, however, the phone rang and she nearly dropped it.

"Hello?"

"Ms. Sloan? This is Charles with Washington Security. Your alarm went off. Are you all right?"

"Y-yes, but—"

"Is there an intruder?"

"I don't know. I didn't hear anything but the alarm."

"I'm calling the police," he told her. "I'll stay on the line with you until help arrives."

Shaken, listening to the old building creak in the night, Mackenzie had never been so scared in her life. She wanted to turn on a light, but every instinct she had told her to wait—there was protection in the dark. If someone had broken in, they could be crazy enough to still be in the shop. Did they know she was there? Had they heard her answer the call from the security company? She'd kept her voice to a whisper, but sounds carried easily in the darkness.

Hugging herself, she was shaking with fear and there didn't seem to be anything she could do to stop it. Then she heard the sirens in the distance. Within seconds, two patrol cars raced down the street and braked to a stop in front of the shop.

Mackenzie didn't wait to see more. Blindly grabbing her robe in the dark, she ran downstairs.

Still half-asleep, Patrick scowled when he recognized Devin's number on his cell phone ID. "Do you have any idea what the hell time it is? What's wrong?"

"I just got a call from dispatch," he growled. "The security alarm at Mackenzie Sloan's shop went off about ten minutes ago. I thought you'd want to know."

Already reaching for his pants, Patrick swore. "Is she there? Dammit, she's all right, isn't she?"

"As far as I know," he said. "I didn't get any details, just that her alarm went off. Are you going over there?"

Stepping into his shoes, he said, "I'm on my way right now." Ten seconds later, the door to his apartment slammed behind him as he ran to his car.

She was all right, he told himself as he hit the Beltway and headed for the Capitol Hill area of Washington. He'd checked out the door to her shop and it was rock solid. She'd had the locks changed, and without the key, no intruder was going to get inside with anything short of a bazooka.

If, he reminded himself, there even was an intruder. The alarm could have possibly malfunctioned or she may have set the damn thing wrong. Maybe the electricity had gone out and her back-up battery was dead. There could be any number of reasons...

But even as he tried to come up with other reasons, his mind was drawing a blank. Then he turned the corner onto her street and saw her standing in her night-clothes in the glare of the patrol car headlights. Armed with a musket—a *musket,* for God's sake!—she stood defiantly in front of her shop, just daring so much as a shadow to move in the darkness of the night.

Relieved, Patrick almost laughed. Damn, she was something! Any other woman would have been cowering in one of the patrol cars with all doors shut and locked, but not Mackenzie Sloan. She stood there with the fire of outrage in her eyes and looked like she not only was prepared to defend herself, if necessary, but that she actually knew how to use the damn musket!

Grinning at the thought, he didn't have to hear the alarm bells clanging in his head to know that she was the kind of woman who could, with very little effort, make him forget the past, forget Carla, forget all the reasons why he'd vowed to never get seriously involved with a woman again. If he was smart, he told himself, he'd leave her in the very capable hands of D.C.'s finest just as soon as he assured himself that she was all right.

But even as he quickly parked and stepped out of his car, he knew there was something about her that he just couldn't walk away from. Especially when he caught sight of the traces of fear hiding behind the flashing defiance in her blue eyes.

Blinded by the headlights of the patrol car, she whirled at the sound of his footsteps on the pavement as he strode toward her. "Who's there?" she gasped, jerking up the musket.

Stepping into the glaring light of the headlights, he held up his hands in surrender and grinned. "Hold your fire, Annie Oakley. I'm unarmed."

Surprised, she almost dropped her musket. "Patrick! What are you doing here?"

"Devin called me," he said as his long legs quickly ate up the distance between them. "He got a call from dispatch when your security company called in. Are you all right?"

Her chin came up at that. "Of course. I can take care of myself."

A crooked grin curled the corner of his mouth. "I never doubted it for a minute. Does that thing even work?"

A sheepish smile curled the corners of her mouth. "No, but the bad guys don't know that. And I wasn't going to stand out here by myself without some kind of weapon while the cops searched the building."

"I should have known." He laughed, and very carefully took the gun from her and laid it on the hood of one of the patrol cars. Sobering as he turned back to her, he said, "What happened? Did someone break in?"

Shivering as a cold, wet wind suddenly swirled around them, she shoved her hands deep in the pockets of her robe. "Not that I know of. When the alarm went off and woke me, I grabbed my gun and ran downstairs the second the police got here. The front door was still locked."

"What about the back door? Or the lower floor windows? I know they're all locked, but they're old. If someone was determined to get in, it wouldn't take much to jimmy one open."

Pale, without an ounce of color in her face, she shivered. "I didn't take time to check anything. I just wanted out of there."

"And you didn't hear anything besides the alarm? No one running into things downstairs in the dark?"

Mutely, she shook her head, and Patrick could only imagine what she must have felt when the screaming alarm woke her. She'd already proven she was a woman who could take care of herself and handle whatever life threw at her, but he'd seen the vulnerable side of her and he knew she wasn't nearly as tough as she pretended.

Even as he watched, the invisible armor she wore cracked ever so slightly and she shivered with fear. Patrick didn't remember moving, didn't remember reaching for her. His only thought to comfort her, he cupped her face in the palm of his hand. Just that quickly, heat lightning set the air between them sizzling.

She felt it as surely as he did. Her eyes, dark with startled awareness, flew to his, and for a second, he swore he could see all the way to her soul. Entranced, he couldn't move, couldn't think, couldn't feel anything but the wild beating of his heart and the intoxicating softness of her skin.

Then, with no warning, the two officers investigating her shop stepped outside and headed toward them, and the spell was broken. Swallowing a silent curse, he dropped his hand and quickly stepped back.

If the two men noticed their closeness—or the tension that had set the air humming between them—they gave no sign of it. Not surprisingly, Patrick recognized them both—with all the family connections in law enforcement, there were few people in the local police and the ranks of the FBI that the O'Reillys didn't know.

Not surprised to see him, Jackson White extended his hand for a quick shake and lifted a grizzled brow. "Devin called you?"

Patrick nodded. "There's a good chance this has something to with some thefts at the Archives."

"Did you discover where the break-in was?" Mackenzie asked.

"There wasn't a break-in," Rick Sanchez retorted, and held up a plastic evidence bag so she could see the key they'd found in the lock. "Someone obviously didn't know you'd changed the locks."

Watching Mackenzie, Patrick would have sworn that every drop of blood drained from her face. She couldn't seem to take her eyes off the key. "Were you able to find any prints?" he asked Jackson.

"No," he said in disgust. "The door was clean, so he must have worn gloves—he didn't have time to wipe it down when the alarm when off."

"And since he didn't manage to actually break in or steal anything," his partner said, "there's—"

"Not much you can do," Mackenzie finished for him. "Too bad, so sad. Is that what you're telling me?"

"No crime's been committed," Jackson said. "We'd

help if we could, but there's nothing anyone can do until this jackass actually does something illegal."

Mackenzie knew they were right, but when they told her to call if she had any more problems, then wished her good-night, she could already feel the fear creeping in, chilling her to the bone. Now what?

Within seconds, the neighborhood was once again quiet and deserted. Up and down the street, Christmas lights twinkled in the darkness, giving a Norman Rockwell feel to the street, but she no longer trusted the peacefulness of the night. Danger lurked in the shadows, watching her.

Hugging herself, Mackenzie glanced up at Patrick. "Tell me the truth. You think it was him, don't you?"

He didn't pretend to misunderstand who *him* was. "Yes."

"But why? He got the receipts."

"Maybe that's not all he was after," he pointed out. At her startled look, he said, "I'm not trying to scare you, Mackenzie, but there's a possibility that your father bought more stolen items from this jackass than we both thought, and that's what he's looking for."

"What? You said there were only twenty documents—the ones I sold on eBay!"

"No," he corrected her, "I said the items you sold on eBay were stolen from the Archives. Since they weren't inventoried, it's impossible to know how many more were stolen...or how many of the stolen items your father actually bought."

"Oh, God." Stricken, she looked at the shop with eyes dark with fear. "If he's really afraid the things my father bought can be traced back to him, he'll be back to get them all. And I don't even know what my father bought! I have no receipts."

"It doesn't matter. We'll take care of it," he promised her, and was stunned to hear those words coming out of his mouth.

What the hell was he doing? Every time his eyes met hers, the kiss was between them. The only one they'd shared, the one he couldn't forget. The one that throbbed with heat and made him want to reach for her and pull her back into his arms every time she got within touching distance.

He had to be losing his mind.

Even as he silently acknowledged that, he couldn't take back his offer. Not when she was in danger and needed his help.

"I have no intention of leaving you to go through this alone," he assured her. "I'll help you. We'll go through everything. Between the two of us, we should have some answers by the end of the week."

Hesitating, she knew she should have said no. He was too easy to turn to, too easy to depend on, too easy to dream about. He tempted her to forget the past and all her fears, and that shook her to the core. She couldn't afford to go there with him.

Like it or not, however, she needed him. Whoever had tried to break in would be back, and next time, he might not let a locked door stop him. Next time, he might come in the middle of the day when the shop was open and he could just walk right in. All he had to do was check to make sure there were no other customers, lock the door behind him and pull out a knife or gun. Once he retrieved the incriminating documents he'd sold to her father, he would, if he had any sense, eliminate any witnesses.

Nerves knotted her stomach at the thought. And for the first time in her life, she was truly afraid. "Okay," she sighed. "When do you want to get started?"

He shrugged. "I'm game when you are. If you want to go back to bed, I can come back later. Or we can get started now. It's your call."

She'd only been asleep four hours when the security alarm had gone off, and any reasonable person would have been exhausted. But just the thought of lying in the dark, listening to the wind moan outside and her old building creak, turned her blood cold.

Shivering, she said huskily, "If you don't mind, I'd rather start now, if that's all right with you."

"No problem," he said easily. "Where do you want to start?"

"The kitchen," she said promptly. "I need some coffee, the stronger the better."

Chapter 6

Armed with coffee that was strong enough to strip paint off metal, they moved into the reading room and stood side by side, surveying the shop. The bookshelves and glass display cases that lined the walls and spilled into the rest of the downstairs public rooms were packed with thousand of items that had taken Mackenzie's father a lifetime to acquire. And they had to go through them one by one. It was a daunting task.

Far from intimidated, Patrick moved to the display case to his right. "We might as well get started. Look for file notes, tear marks, anything that looks like it was an official government document."

"My father would have known to look for all that," she argued. "You're not going to find anything like that."

"I hope not," he said honestly. "But whoever showed

up at your door with a key tonight was after something, Mac. We just have to figure out what it was."

That was easier said than done. For the next two hours, they went through everything in the front room, and the first thing Mackenzie found was an eighteenth-century sketch pad of William Thornton, the designer of the U.S. Capitol. There were no markings to indicate that it had once been in the National Archives, but Mackenzie's heart sank at the sight of it. How could her father not have realized that it was probably stolen? The sketch pad was filled with architectural drawings of the Capitol in various stages of construction!

"What did you find?" Patrick asked, appearing at her side.

Without a word, she handed it to him.

"It could have been privately owned," he told her quietly as he examined it. "Thornton probably filled numerous sketch pads with his designs before he came up with the plans that he turned in to the government."

Mackenzie knew that was a possibility, and she appreciated the fact that he tried to make her feel better, but it didn't help. "Even so, he should have gotten some kind of documentation proving that," she argued. "He always did in the past. When I was a kid, he was a real stickler for that kind of thing. People came up to him at shows all the time with the most incredible maps and books, wanting him to buy them, and he never would. Not without documentation. What happened? Why did he stop being so careful?"

"He got older," Patrick said, squeezing her shoulder consolingly. "And sick. Look around, sweetheart. It's obvious the business got to be too much for him. He was tired and sick and probably just not thinking clearly."

"I should have been here," she said huskily, blinking back tears. "He needed me and I wasn't here."

"Stop that," he chided. "You had a right to your own life. Nobody would blame you for that, certainly not your father. We all have a right to do our own thing.

"And," he added, setting the sketch pad on the front counter, "you don't know what his real intentions were. For all we know, he bought them so they couldn't be sold to a private collector and disappear forever. He may have intended to turn them in to the Archives and just never got around to it."

That was about as implausible a scenario as Mackenzie had ever heard. Amusement drying the last of her tears, she looked up at him with a grin. "Excuse me. Did I hear you correctly? Did those words really come out of the mouth of Special Agent I'm-Going-To-Hound-You-Until-You-Fess-Up O'Reilly?"

A sheepish grin curled the corners of his mouth. "Okay, so you caught me. I confess. I'm a softie sometimes. Catch me on the right day, and I even believe in Santa Claus."

"Be still my heart," she teased. And giving in to impulse, she turned to him, stood on tiptoe and surprised them both with a whisper-soft kiss.

She didn't know it, but she could have pushed Patrick over with a feather. Stunned, delighted, he just barely stopped himself from reaching for her when she stepped back. "What was that for?" he asked huskily.

"For you being such a nice guy," she said simply. "And because I could."

She started to turn away, but not before he caught sight of her flirty grin. Lightning quick, he reached for her. "Whoa, not so fast, sassy," he said with a grin, turning her back to face him. "I see who you are now. You're one of those women who takes advantage of a man when he drops his guard and makes the mistake of showing you his soft, vulnerable underbelly, aren't you?"

Her eyes wide and innocent—and dancing with mischief—she sniffed. "I have no idea what you're talking about."

"Really?" he drawled. "Maybe I should show you."

Laughing, she snatched free of his hold and danced away. "Oh, no, you don't. We have work to do, remember? And I'm counting on you to catch the big bad wolf for me."

"Okay," he groaned. "Be that way. But if you ever change your mind, all you have to do is tell me. You can take advantage of me anytime you want."

Watching heat singe her cheeks, Patrick told himself he was just teasing, just giving her back some of her own, but the little voice inside his head wasn't buying it. *Yeah, right. She knocked you out of your shoes the second you laid eyes on her, and you know it. And the more you get to know her, the more smitten you are. Where do you think this is going, bucko?*

He didn't have an answer for that, didn't want one. "Time to get back to work," he said gruffly. "I'm going to start on the maps."

Flushed, her heart threatening to beat right out of her breast, Mackenzie couldn't remember the last time a man had flustered her so. She certainly hadn't felt that

way with Hugh—they had been friends who had slowly
evolved into lovers, and although she would have sworn
she loved him, there'd been no fireworks between them.
In the course of their two-year relationship, she'd never
found herself daydreaming about him in the middle of
the day, unconsciously looking for him in a crowd,
lying awake at night, thinking about him, unable to get
him out of her head…like she did Patrick.

Stunned by the direction of her thoughts, she nearly
dropped a well-kept, leather-bound volume that was in
amazingly good shape despite its apparent age. Gasping,
she caught it and hardly spared it a glance as she set it
on top of a pile of other books she'd removed from the
shelves to inspect. Then, with a will of their own, her
eyes jumped back to the book she'd just added to the pile.

It was old—very old—with no writing on the spine
or front of the book. Puzzled, she opened it to the cover
page and nearly dropped it again. A strong, old-fash-
ioned hand that had faded to sienna declared the book
to be the personal property of General George Washington. It was dated December, 1777.

Stunned, Mackenzie couldn't take her eyes from the
familiar bold signature. Valley Forge. The book was
Washington's diary at Valley Forge. And there was no
question that it belonged in the National Archives and that
her father would have known that. He'd bought it anyway.

"Patrick."

That was all she said, just his name, but something in
her tone must have hinted at the despair she was feeling.
He turned, took one look at her face, and was at her side
in four long strides. "What is it? What's wrong?"

"It's Washington's diary at Valley Forge," she said hollowly.

Swearing, Patrick could only imagine what she was feeling. The father she had loved and trusted all her life was not the man she'd thought he was.

His heart aching for her, he carefully took the book from her, set it aside and couldn't stop himself from pulling her into his arms. "It may not be what you think," he murmured, cradling her close. "There could be another explanation."

"What?" she asked huskily, pulling back to gaze up at him with blue eyes swimming in tears. "What other explanation could there be? My father did research at the Archives for years. He knew what belonged there and what didn't. I don't care how sick he was, he wouldn't have bought this by mistake. It's Washington's private diary at Valley Forge, for God's sake!"

If the situation hadn't been so serious, he would have smiled at her indignant tone. At least her tears had vanished. "We don't know what your father was thinking or how he ended up with the diary," he pointed out. "There's so much stuff in here that I don't know how he could have possibly known everything in his inventory. Maybe he bought some things in lot at an auction and just stuck everything on the shelf when he brought it back to the shop."

"He wouldn't have done that."

"He might not have done it when he was younger," he agreed, "but people change when they get old and sick. I'm not saying your father was a bad man, but he wasn't the same man when he died as he was when you were a child. And the point is, it doesn't matter. He got that book from someone, the same someone who, in all likelihood, tried to get in your shop this morning. *This* may just be what they came back for."

Mackenzie had to admit that if she had been in the thief's shoes, the diary would have been something she would definitely have come back for. It was extremely valuable…and not something that the average collector would have come across at an estate sale or even at a memorabilia show. There had to be a record of it and when it went missing.

"So what do we do now?" she asked. "Whoever sold this to Dad knows the locks and the alarm code have been changed. The odds are they're not going to try to break in again. So how are we going to catch them? We still don't have a clue who they are."

"We'll figure something out," he promised her, "as soon as we finish going through the rest of your father's things. Right now, though, we could both use a break. C'mon, let's go to breakfast."

Fifteen minutes later, when they stepped into a diner two blocks down the street from the Capitol, Mackenzie wasn't surprised to discover that the place was already filling up fast in spite of the fact that it was barely six in the morning. Quickly snagging the only unoccupied booth left, they had hardly settled into their seats when a harried waitress presented them with menus and coffee before hurrying away to another table.

Looking around, Mackenzie was grateful for the

hustle and bustle of the morning crowd. After the drama of the previous two hours, this was just what she needed. Bacon and eggs and coffee. Nothing else. No worries about how her father had come into the possession of the stolen items. No second thoughts about how she'd once again ended up in Patrick's arms. There was only now, this moment, and breakfast to concern herself with. Nothing else.

Satisfied that she had everything under control, she settled back to enjoy her coffee while they waited for the waitress to make her way back to them. Then Patrick's foot accidentally grazed hers under the table as he stretched out his long legs in an attempt to get more comfortable in the small booth. In the time it took to blink, all her attention was focused on him.

Don't be an idiot, she ordered herself sternly as her heart quickened. He wasn't flirting. He wasn't even looking at her. Instead, his attention was completely focused on the menu.

As, she silently admitted, hers should have been. But it had been a long, emotional night, she was tired, and her defenses were down. And somehow, when she wasn't looking, Patrick had slipped past her guard into her life.

He was just…a *friend,* she decided. Well, sort of. If, she thought ruefully, you could call someone who initially wanted to put you in jail, then later kissed the stuffing out of you, a friend.

She wished he'd kiss her again.

Stiffening, she told herself not to go there, but it was too late for that. Her gaze lifted to the sensuous curve of his mouth, only to have the bottom of her stomach fall away with longing. Just once more, she told herself. She ached for him to kiss her just one more time…just to see if it was as intoxicating as she remembered.

Across the diner, a man barked with laughter at something his companion said, bringing Mackenzie back to her surroundings with a start. When Patrick glanced up at her at the same time, her cheeks flushed with hot color. She blushed like a sixteen-year-old.

"My God, you're blushing!"

"Don't be silly. I just—"

"What?" he teased when she hesitated. "Can't take your eyes off me?"

"Of course not! You're delusional—"

"I don't think so."

"I just—"

"Don't stop now. You just what? Go ahead. Spill your guts. I can't wait to hear what you're thinking."

If he thought he had her, he was in for a rude awakening. Quickly collecting herself, she smiled sweetly and reached across the table to trail a finger across the back of his hand. "What I think is you can be quite appealing when you want to be. You're just so…manly."

He burst out laughing and caught her wayward finger before she could draw it back. "Manly, huh?"

"I can't take my eyes off you."

His eyes dancing, he grinned. "Uh-huh. And you expect me to believe that?"

"Well, of course." Turning her hand in his, she teasingly caressed his palm. "Why wouldn't you? You're fascinating. And—"

When her grin broadened, he knew he was in trouble. "Why do I have a feeling my ego's about to get flattened?"

"I don't know," she said innocently. "I was just going to say you're a halfway decent kisser, too."

He straightened at that. "I beg your pardon?"

"That's important, you know," she said with a straight face and dancing eyes. "A man can make up for a lot of character flaws by being a good kisser."

"So now you're saying I have character flaws?"

She shrugged lightly. "It's unfortunate, but we all have them—some people more than others. So I'd keep working on my kissing if I were you. Just in case."

Laughing, he raised her hand to his lips and pressed a lingering kiss to her palm. "How's that?"

Mackenzie felt the heat of that kiss all the way to her toes, and realized, too late, that she was out of her league. Still, she had no intention of letting him know that. "Not bad," she said with a faint smile. "A little predictable, though."

Not the least bit insulted, he chuckled. "It looks like I underestimated you, Ms. Sloan. Congratulations. I don't do that very often."

Grinning, she said, "You deserved that. You're a terrible pest."

"Thank you," he said with a wicked flash of his dimples as the waitress returned to take their order and bring them more coffee. "I try."

Mackenzie had to laugh. "You must have driven your mother crazy when you were a kid."

"I had help. My brothers were the outrageous ones.

And my dad, of course. He was the best. He could make my mom laugh when no one else could."

Sobering, Mackenzie said quietly, "When did he die?"

"When I was eleven," he said gruffly. "He was a traffic cop and got shot when he stopped a speeder who ran a red light. He never knew the bastard had just robbed a convenience store and was high as a kite on cocaine."

"Oh, my God," she gasped softly. "I'm sorry. That must have been horrible for all of you. Especially your mother."

He nodded, his eyes glinting with remembered pain. "They had the best marriage of anyone I've ever known," he said simply. "Dad's been dead for twenty years and she still misses him every day."

"So she never remarried?"

"No. She could never love anyone else. That doesn't mean she didn't have her chances," he added ruefully. "She just never noticed."

Mackenzie grinned, understanding completely. "My dad was the same way. After my mom died, one of the neighbor ladies brought us a casserole every night for a year and Dad never realized she was crazy about him."

"But you did. And you hated her guts."

Surprised, she laughed. "How did you know?"

"Because that's how I felt when guys on the force that had been friends with my dad came sniffing around, trying to convince my mother that she was lonely and needed company." Laughing at the memory, he said, "It was a good thing she wasn't interested because my brothers and I sent them packing. Well, all but Neal, of course."

"Neal?"

"My dad's partner," he replied. "He was there for all

of us after Dad died. I don't know what my mother would have done without him, especially when we all hit our teens. We were pretty wild."

He smiled at the memory, but before he could tell her about some of the outlandish things he and his brothers had done, his cell phone rang. Frowning, he reached for it. "Who would be calling me at this time of the morning?"

Carla O'Reilly.

What the hell! He hadn't heard a word from her in over two years. And even then, she hadn't called to chat, just to make it clear that he was wasting his time and money trying to get visitation rights with Tommy. He wasn't his son and Tommy didn't need him. He had a daddy.

"Patrick?" Mackenzie asked quietly. "Are you all right? Aren't you going to answer it?"

Caught in the sharp-clawed grip of the past, it was several long seconds before he heard her. "What? Oh, yes, of course."

His jaw rigid, he flipped open his phone and growled, "Hello?"

"Daddy?"

Whatever Patrick had been expecting, it wasn't the sound of his son's voice on the other end of the line. Stunned, he nearly dropped the phone. "Hey, sport," he said huskily. "What's going on?"

"Mommy's car won't start. She said I could call you to see if you could take me to school."

"Of course I can," he said promptly, even as alarm bells were clanging wildly in his head. "What time does Mommy usually leave to take you to school?"

"She said if you could be here at eight, that would be fine."

"I'll be there," he promised. "Be ready."

It wasn't until he hung up that he remembered Mackenzie. Swearing, he said, "I'm sorry, Mac. I've got to go. We're going to have to take a rain check on breakfast."

Already gathering up her purse, she said, "Of course. Is something wrong? I can walk home—it's only four blocks."

He gave her a chiding look. "You're not walking home, silly. I'll take you. I'm just sorry that I have to rush you out of here before you have a chance to eat."

"Don't worry about me," she assured him as she slid from the booth and he flagged the waitress down to cancel their order, then gave her a generous tip. "I won't fade away if I miss breakfast."

"I'm not touching that with a ten-foot pole." He chuckled. "C'mon, let's get out of here."

Seconds later, they were rushing back to her shop, and as Mackenzie rode beside him in silence, she could tell his thoughts were on the phone call. Who was he taking to school? Obviously, it was a little boy—he'd called him *sport*. So who was he? A nephew? A friend's son? A *girlfriend's* son? *His* son?

Surprised by the thought, she frowned. He'd never mentioned having any children, but then again, they hadn't actually had a conversation about their private lives. Was he still involved with the mother of his child...if he had a child? She wouldn't have said he was a man who rattled easily, but that phone call appeared to have caught him completely off guard. What was going on?

She wanted to ask, but there was no time. He braked to a stop in front of her shop and immediately apologized again as he came around to open her door for her. "I really am sorry about this. I just have to…take care of something."

And with no other explanation than that, he climbed back into his car and drove off.

Two years had passed since he'd last walked up to the front door of the house he and Carla had shared, and nothing had changed. The same plants were in the flower box, the same curtains at the living room window.

As he strode up the front walk, however, he didn't feel as if he was going home. Instead, he felt as if he was walking into a trap.

For the span of a split second, he seriously considered turning on his heel and getting out of there while he could. Then the front door was jerked open.

"Dad!"

Shooting through the door like a bullet, Tommy launched himself at him. "You came!"

"Well, of course I came." He laughed, and felt his heart clench as he wrapped his arms around his son for the first time in what seemed like forever. He was bigger, taller and had lost the baby fat that had made him look like a cherub. Somehow, the toddler that had been snatched away from him had turned into a rough-and-tumble little boy while he wasn't there to see, and that hurt far more than he'd expected.

"What have you been eating, champ?" he teased, pulling back to look down at him with a grin. "You're nearly as big as I am."

"Mama says I'm going to be taller than you."

Patrick's smile faded. Whatever his son turned out to be—tall, short, curly-haired or straight—it had nothing to do with him. That wasn't something he could tell Tommy, however. Not at this age. He would never understand.

A sound at the door caught his attention, and he looked up sharply to find his ex-wife standing there. For a moment, he thought he saw tears in her eyes, but then she blinked, and he knew he was only kidding himself. The woman who stood looking at him with shuttered eyes was the woman who had divorced him, not the one he'd fallen in love with when he was sixteen years old. That Carla was gone forever, and he was relieved to discover that he no longer had any feelings for the woman she had become…except distrust.

Turning his attention back to Tommy, he set him back on his feet and nudged him gently toward his mother. "Go kiss your mother goodbye and get your backpack, champ. We've got to get going or you're going to be late for school."

He didn't have to tell him twice. Immune to the sudden tension sparking in the air, he ran to his mother, gave her a quick hug and a kiss and grabbed his backpack. "Bye, Mom."

"Have a good day," she called after him as he ran back to Patrick. "I'll be there this afternoon to pick you up. I'll be in Aunt Binky's car. Watch for me."

His smile broad as he slipped his hand into Patrick's, he said, "Okay, Mom," but he never looked back as he tugged Patrick toward his car. "C'mon, Dad, we gotta get doughnuts. 'Member? The little holey things with chocolate inside them? We ate millions of 'em."

"I remember." He chuckled. "You're talking about Lulu's Doughnut Shop."

"Yeah! Can we go? Please? Pleeeze?"

Laughing, Patrick hugged him. "We can do anything you want, sport, as long as you're not late for school."

Thrilled, Tommy chatted happily about school and helping Carla decorate the Christmas tree. Swallowing the lump in his throat as he headed for the doughnut shop, Patrick knew better than to make the mistake of thinking anything had changed. Carla was up to something—there was no doubt about that. Her sister, Bianca, adored Tommy and would have been more than willing to let Carla borrow her car, not only to pick him up from school, but to take him, as well. So why had she had Tommy call him? What kind of game was she playing? And why?

Chapter 7

Later, Patrick couldn't have said what he did after he bought Tommy doughnuts, then dropped him off at school. He didn't know when—if ever—he would see his son again, and it took nothing more than that thought to rip a fresh hole in his heart. Lost, pain clawing at him, he wanted to believe that Carla wasn't that cruel. She wouldn't have invited him into his son's life again just for the span of a ride to school.

Why not? an angry voice in his head demanded. *Forget caring about you. If she'd cared two cents for her son, she would have never denied him a relationship with the only father he'd ever known. Don't underestimate her. She's capable of anything.*

No one knew that better than he. He still bore the emotional scars to prove it.

So why was he letting her tear him apart again? he wondered, furious with himself for letting her manipulate him so easily. She had friends she could have asked to give Tommy a ride to school. Why had she had Tommy call him? Why was she opening that door again? She had to know that if she kicked him out of his son's life a second time, it would destroy him.

Was that her goal? Did she hate him that much? Why? What had he done to her? Granted, he'd fought her for custody and visitation rights during their divorce, but once the judge had ruled he had no rights whatsoever and she threatened to call the cops if he didn't leave her and Tommy alone, he hadn't given her any trouble. He'd turned his back and walked away and learned to live with the fact that he had no son. She'd won. What more did she want from him? He had nothing left to give.

Frustrated, needing to talk to someone, he should have gone over to his mother's or one of his brothers'. But he knew what they would say. *Don't trust her. Don't give her a chance to hurt you again.* And they would be right. But could he pass up the chance to be a part of his son's life, however small that chance might be, and possibly watch him grow up just because Carla might pull the rug out from under him at any time? Could he really do that?

Torn between a commonsense decision and his heart, he drove mindlessly for what seemed like hours and paid little attention to where he drove. It wasn't until he pulled up in front of Mackenzie's shop that he realized he'd been trying to find his way there for hours.

Stunned, he just sat there in front of her shop, wondering when she had become someone he could confide in. After his divorce, he'd sworn he'd never be stupid enough to trust a woman again. When had that changed? What had Mackenzie done to him?

He told himself he didn't need this today, not after Carla had once again found a way to turn his life upside down. But even as he ordered himself to get the hell out of there while he still could, he knew he couldn't. Right or wrong, safe or not, he had to see Mackenzie.

In the process of pouring herself a cup of coffee, Mackenzie straightened in surprise at the sound of John Philip Sousa booming throughout the shop, signaling a customer. Her heart tripped, and for a moment, she found herself hoping it was Patrick. But it had been over three hours since he'd canceled their breakfast together and dropped her off at her shop. She'd half expected him to come back after he rushed off to help the child who'd needed a ride to school, but he hadn't. Was he now helping the child's mother?

Not liking the direction of her thoughts, she jerked herself back to the matter at hand—a customer. "Just look around," she called out. "I'll be right there."

"No hurry," Patrick said from the kitchen doorway. "I've got plenty of time."

Whirling, Mackenzie felt her heart lurch at the sight of him. His green eyes were serious despite his crooked smile, and something told her that whatever errand he'd run that morning had not been easy for him. He looked…hurt, grim, older.

Concerned, she wanted to ask him what was wrong,

but heard herself say, instead, "You look like a man who missed breakfast."

Surprised, he laughed. "Actually, now that you mention it, I did—though I did have a few doughnut holes. What about you?"

"I wasn't really hungry," she admitted honestly. "Have a seat. I'll whip you up something."

"Oh, no, you don't. I owe you breakfast."

"So I'll collect another time," she said with a shrug. "It's a little late for breakfast, but I've got bacon and eggs, if you like. Or we can have lunch. There's baked chicken, chili, soup, homemade bread. Name your poison."

She wasn't taking no for answer, and they both knew it. Studying her, he lifted a dark brow. "Is the soup homemade?"

Grinning, she nodded. "My grandmother's chicken noodle recipe."

"Really? And you make it as well as your grandmother did?"

"Better. I make my own homemade noodles."

"Well, that settles it," he said promptly. "Soup it is… and a chicken sandwich. What do you want me to do?"

"Set the table and slice the bread while I heat the soup. What do you want on your sandwich?"

"Everything but the kitchen sink."

"Okay." She laughed and started pulling items out of the refrigerator.

Ten minutes later, when they sat down across from each other at her small kitchen table, Mackenzie silently admitted that she could get used to having a man's help in the kitchen. Especially a man like Patrick. He obviously knew his way around a kitchen and hadn't once asked her where things were or what he could do next. He found everything he needed, and by the time she heated the soup and sliced the chicken for sandwiches, simple soup and sandwiches had turned into a feast.

"I'm impressed," she told him. "You're very handy in the kitchen."

"Are you kidding? You're the cook. I just cleaned out your refrigerator. If it tastes as good as it smells…"

"It does," she retorted, grinning. "No bragging, just fact."

"Yeah, yeah, that's what they all say," he teased as he dipped his spoon into the soup. "It'll have to be pretty darn good to beat my mother's."

Her eyes twinkling with amusement, Mackenzie didn't say a word as he carefully brought a spoonful of soup to his mouth. Five seconds later, he looked like a man who'd just been struck by lightning. "Will you marry me?"

Mackenzie laughed, not the least surprised by his reaction. "I take it you like it."

"Are you sure you won't marry me? We could sell this to Campbell's and make a fortune."

"We?"

"Okay, so we'll have a prenuptial. You can have all the money since it's your grandmother's recipe…and pay all the bills."

"Really?" She laughed. "Then what do I need you for?"

When he just looked at her, she giggled. "You're outrageous. Stop that."

"You asked," he said with a wicked grin. "Frankly, I thought you were smarter than that—did you just throw a chip at me?"

Not the least repentant, she teased, "I thought *you* were smarter than that, but if you have to ask…"

For an answer, he threw a chip at her, and the war was on.

Laughing, Mackenzie knew she couldn't win. He came from a family of boys who had, no doubt, been incredibly competitive—and probably still were. He wasn't a man who would accept defeat easily.

That didn't mean, however, that she folded her tent and called it a day. She liked to think she gave as good as she got, and when they both ran out of chips, they were both laughing so hard, they could hardly catch their breath. And for the first time since Patrick had appeared at her kitchen door, he looked like his old self. His smile was real, his eyes full of mischief and whatever tension he'd brought back with him from his morning errand was long gone.

"You look better," she said as he helped her clean up the mess they'd made. "Did you have a difficult morning?"

Glancing up from the potato chips he was sweeping up, he blinked in surprise. "How did you know?"

"Your eyes. You looked…weary," she said, "almost as if you were beaten down. Not that you have to tell me about it," she added quickly when he started to respond. "It's not any of my business. I was just concerned."

"I—"

"Obviously, you took someone to school, and it was someone you cared about, but it's not any of my—"

"Business," he finished for her, smiling. "You already said that, Mac."

"I know. I'm sorry," she said huskily as she turned away to begin clearing the table. "It really is none of—"

"Your business," he finished for her again, his smile broadening into a grin. "I think we've established that. But that's not going to stop me from telling you about it."

"It's not?"

"I spent the last three hours driving all over D.C. and Virginia trying to figure some things out," he said huskily. "And when I wasn't paying any attention, my car led me back here to you. I need to talk to someone, and apparently, you're it…if that's okay with you."

Touched, she found herself blinking back tears. "Of course. You can tell me anything you like."

So just that easily, Mackenzie found herself once again seated across the kitchen table from him. But when he began to talk, he didn't tell her about that morning or the child he'd given a ride to school. Instead, he told her about the past…and an old love.

"I met Carla for the first time when she was fourteen and I was sixteen. We had each gone to the movies with separate friends and found ourselves standing in line together at the concession stand."

His eyes trained on a memory Mackenzie couldn't see, he admitted, "I'd never met anyone who'd knocked me out of my shoes before. She was beautiful and smart and like a sap, I fell in love with her without knowing a damn thing about her."

"And her parents let her date at fourteen?" Mackenzie asked in surprise.

"No, but that didn't stop Carla. She would sneak out…or lie about where she was going and meet me at the mall. It was all completely innocent, and it only lasted a month. Then her father was transferred to New York," he said flatly, "and that was that."

Mackenzie didn't believe for a second that the story ended there, not when his eyes were dark with an old, remembered pain. Too late, however, she discovered she didn't want to hear the rest of the story, didn't want to know any more about the brazen Carla who had broken his heart long before Mackenzie had ever met him. It hurt too much. *He* hurt too much, and every instinct she possessed warned her that the worst of the story was yet to come.

But the dam had broken, and there was no holding the words back. His face carved in harsh lines, he said, "Then she moved back to D.C. three years after I graduated from college."

"And you got back together," she said quietly.

His gaze focused on the past, he nodded. "Looking back on it, I was really stupid. I'd never forgotten her, and when I saw her again, I fell in love with her all over again. Like a fool, though, I didn't protect myself or her. Three months later, she was pregnant and we were getting married."

"So the little boy you took to school this morning was your son?" When he glanced at her in quick surprise, she said, "I couldn't help but overhear. You called him sport."

"His name's Tommy," he told her. "But he's not my son."

Confused, she frowned. "But I thought you said—"

"Carla lied," he said flatly. "She really was pregnant. But not with my child."

Shocked, Mackenzie could only imagine what that had felt like. "Oh, Patrick! That must have been horrible. Are you sure she wasn't just saying that out of spite? People say horrible things in a divorce."

"The judge who presided over our divorce ordered a DNA test," he said bitterly. "There's no mistake. I'm not Tommy's father."

"Except in every other way that counts," she pointed out. "How old was he when you found out?"

"Three," he said gruffly.

"Three!" She choked, outraged. "She waited three years to tell you the truth?!"

He nodded grimly. "She'd run into Tommy's father and realized he was the man she really loved. She wanted to see if they could make it—for Tommy's sake."

"And what about you?"

"I wasn't allowed to see him," he retorted. "I wasn't his father."

Just thinking about it had the old, familiar anger twisting in his gut. "If anyone had told me when I fell in love with her that she could be that vindictive, I would have called them a flat-out liar. But she cut me out of her and Tommy's life like I never existed. Until this morning, I hadn't spoken to either one of them for over two years."

Shocked, Mackenzie gasped, "How could she do that to a three-year-old? That poor baby! Can you imagine how confused he must have been? One day, Daddy's there, and the next, he never sees him again."

"Until today."

Unable to sit still, he rose to his feet to prowl restlessly around the kitchen. "I don't know what the hell she's up to," he growled. "Why, after two years, would she suddenly need me to take Tommy to school? She has friends she could have called. Hell, she could have called a cab and taken him herself."

"Obviously, she's changed her mind about letting you see him, at least for now," Mackenzie said. "The question is why. What do you think is going on?"

"I wish to hell I knew," he retorted, dragging a hand through his hair. "I hate it when things don't make sense. And nothing about this makes sense. Tommy's been weaned away from me—he's adjusted to not having me in his life. So why drag me back into the picture?"

"She's got to know that's not good for Tommy," Mackenzie pointed out. "You're either his father or you're not. You're either in his life or you're not. Surely she knows she can't have it both ways."

"Oh, she knows," he said grimly. "She's not a dumb woman or an indifferent mother. She kicked me out of Tommy's life because she didn't want him to have any confusion about who his father was."

"And what about his biological father? Is he still in the picture?"

He shrugged. "I have no idea."

Sitting back in her seat, Mackenzie studied him. "So what are you going to do if you have the opportunity to see him again?"

There'd been a time when Patrick wouldn't have hesitated at the chance to see his son. But now he wasn't nearly so sure that would be the right thing to do. Not that he didn't still love him, he assured himself. He didn't care what the DNA results were or what Carla said and a judge ruled—Tommy was and always would be his son. But everything inside him twisted at the thought of losing him again.

"I don't know," he said honestly. "I wasn't ready to get married the day Carla told me she was pregnant, but I was thrilled at the thought of being a dad. My father was fantastic, and for three years, I had the same relationship with Tommy that my dad had with me. Then Carla took that all away and I was forced to accept the fact that as much as I loved him, Tommy wasn't my son. And he never will be."

"Which means Carla has all the power," Mackenzie said. "She can jerk you around like a puppet if she wants to. You have to decide if you want to let her."

His mouth flattened into a grim line. "Exactly. And right now, I don't have a clue what I'm going to do."

Her heart breaking for him, Mackenzie had never seen a man who looked so lonely. "This must be a nightmare for you. I wish there was something I could do to help."

His smile a rueful grimace, he said, "You let me dump all this on you and never voiced a word of complaint. And that was *after* I stood you up for breakfast. Most women would have told me to take a hike."

"I'm not most women."

He was, Patrick silently acknowledged, discovering that for himself. And she had no idea how she fascinated him and scared the hell out of him at one and the same time. At some point, he knew he was going to have to decide how he really felt about her, but for the moment, they both had another problem to deal with.

"No, you're not," he agreed. "I accused you of selling stolen documents, and what do you do? Help me search your shop for hot stuff your dad bought."

"Well, what else was I supposed to do?" she said wryly. "I had to clear my dad's name."

"You could have called your lawyer," he pointed out. "She wouldn't have let me anywhere near your shop without a search warrant."

"What would have been the point of that? You would have gotten it eventually, and I would still have to clear my dad's name."

"Sweetheart, we've only gone through part of the shop," he reminded her. "There could still be something in here that incriminates your father."

Not the least concerned, she dismissed his words with a wave of her hand. "You can forget that. Ask anyone who knew my dad and they'll all tell you the same thing. He was as honest as the day is long. Stealing just wasn't in his DNA."

"That may be," he agreed, "but there's still no explanation for how he ended up with Washington's Valley Forge diary. Not to mention," he added, "the playbill from Ford's Theatre and the other items you found here in the shop and sold on eBay. I understand you loved your dad, Mac, but these things didn't just walk in here by themselves. If your dad didn't steal them, then he had to be doing business with someone who did."

He had her there and they both knew it. Her shoulders

slumping in defeat, she sighed. "I know. And I wasn't around him enough over the last few years to know what was going on with the business. When he talked, we usually talked about personal things—old friends, plans for the weekend, conferences he was planning to attend. He never mentioned any of his business associates—or customers, for that matter—by name."

Frowning, he swore softly. "Damn, we need those receipts! Even if the thief used an alias, we probably could still trace him. But with no paperwork, we've got nothing to go on."

"So how do we set up a sting when we don't know where to begin?"

"We could put the diary on eBay," he said, "but then, we could end up dealing with hundreds of prospective buyers and not have a clue if any of them were the real thief."

Mackenzie agreed. "The thief knows the value of that diary. If he spies it on eBay, he's going to smell a trap. That's not where you sell something like that. What about *The Patriot?*"

The weekly conservative newspaper was published in Concord, Massachusetts, and had an impressive circulation. There were no classifieds, per se, but occasionally, rare items of historical significance were discreetly placed in the paper for sale.

"That's a great idea!" Patrick said, pleased. "It's common knowledge in the business that you're already eliminating inventory, so he won't be surprised when he sees the ad in *The Patriot.* It's where true collectors look for authentic, one-of-a-kind items."

"But this isn't a collector," she pointed out. "He's a thief. Why would he be crazy enough to buy something he's already sold once? He'd be taking a huge risk, wouldn't he?"

"It's hot," he reminded her. "Trust me, he wants it back."

"But why? What will he do with it?"

"Make it disappear, then do everything he can to make sure he's not connected to the theft," he said promptly. "And it's not just the diary you have to worry about, Mac. It's *everything* this man sold your dad, everything that can be traced back to him. He can't take a chance that anything else surfaces on eBay or anywhere else."

"Which is why we have to find it all *before* the jackass comes back for it," she said flatly.

"Exactly. So where do you want to start? On the second floor or in the attic?"

"The attic," she said promptly. "I haven't stepped foot in there since Dad died—with everything else I had to do, I couldn't make myself go up there. It was packed to the rafters when I was a little girl, and I don't imagine that's changed. Dad wasn't one to throw things out."

That proved to be a huge understatement. Five minutes later, when Mackenzie stepped into the attic and Patrick followed her inside, he understood perfectly why she had yet to tackle cleaning the place out. It was huge— and packed with a lifetime of historical treasures and junk that her father had, no doubt, forgotten he even had.

"Where did all this stuff come from?"

"Everywhere!" Mackenzie groaned. "Did I forget to mention that when I was a little girl, Dad used to collect everything and anything connected to the Civil War? We went all the way to Georgia one time for a saddle that had supposedly belonged to Robert E. Lee."

"You've got to be kidding."

"I think there's some cannonballs in here, too. And a couple of spyglasses." Her blue eyes twinkling with mischief, she said, "Those were pretty handy to have around. I used to spy on the neighbors with them."

"See, that's the difference between boys and girls," he teased. "All you wanted to do was watch the neighbors so you'd have something to gossip about. My brothers and I would have had our own war games with all this stuff."

"And blown up the neighborhood in the process," she said dryly. "Your mother was probably white-headed by the time she was thirty."

Grinning, he didn't deny it. "We made life…interesting."

"You mean you were holy terrors."

"The O'Reilly brothers?" he scoffed. "I have no idea what you're talking about. We were model children."

"Yeah, right." She chuckled. "At least you appeared to outgrow it. I guess I can trust you with the cannonballs."

Glancing back at the dust-covered items that were stacked to the ceiling, he said dryly, "I don't think you have anything to worry about. By the time I find them, I'll be too old to pick them up."

Chapter 8

Six hours later, as the last of the light faded from the western sky and streetlights sprang on all over the city, they finally finished their search. And to Mackenzie's relief, they didn't find as many stolen items as she'd feared. There was a letter from President Lincoln to General Grant at the height of the Civil War, several maps from the Lewis and Clark expedition and, of all things, a hand-written copy of FDR's address to the nation after the Japanese attack on Pearl Harbor. With the things they'd found that morning, there were fewer than a dozen documents at the shop that belonged in the Archives.

Relieved, Mackenzie didn't know if she wanted to laugh or cry. "Now what?"

For an answer, Patrick ran a finger down her nose and

held it up for her to see the dust he'd wiped off her. "What do you think?"

Far from embarrassed, she only grinned. "It looks like somebody needs a bath. How'd you get so dirty?"

"Me? You're the one with dirt on your face."

"Really?" Following his lead, she ran a finger down his nose, then held it up for him to see. "I'd say that's a case of the pot calling the kettle black."

"And your point is?"

"We both need a shower."

"I agree," he retorted, and grabbed her hand. "C'mon, let's go. I'll scrub your back and you can scrub mine."

Laughing, she tugged at her hand as he tugged her down the attic stairs after him. "Stop! Are you crazy? We can't take a shower together."

"Why not?" he demanded as they reached the second floor. "Think of it as water conservation. Two for the price of one. The city water board will commend you."

"No!" she said sternly, then ruined it with a giggle. "I mean it."

"You think I'll look, don't you? I won't. I promise. Scout's honor."

His green eyes alight with wicked humor, he grinned down at her, just daring her to say yes, and had no idea just how badly she wanted to do exactly that. It would be so easy. *He* would make it easy…and that's where the danger lay. With just a kiss, he could make her forget her own name. If she ever made the mistake of letting it go beyond that, he could make her forget all her fears, and that was something she couldn't allow him or any other man to do.

Her smile fading, she tightened her fingers around his and fought the sudden crazy need to cry. "I can't," she said huskily.

Another man might have pushed her. After all, even she could hear the longing in her voice. But as she watched his eyes turn dark with a heat he made no effort to hide, he took her at her word. "Okay," he rasped. "We'll save the shower for another time. But not the kiss."

"Patrick—"

That was all he gave her time to say—just his name—then he was reaching for her, pulling her into his arms and covering her mouth with his. She should have pulled back, should have reminded herself why this wasn't smart, should have done anything but kiss him back. But he held her as if he was never going to let her go and kissed her with a hunger that lit a hot fire low in her belly, and all she could think was...more. She wanted, needed, *ached* for more. With a soft, nearly soundless moan, she crowded closer.

Caught up in the heat of her, Patrick tried to remind himself that he'd promised her just a kiss. *One* kiss. One that wouldn't lead to anything but a husky good-night and a lonely drive home.

It should have been easy. He'd perfected that kind of kiss when he was sixteen years old. After all these years, he could do it without even thinking about it.

Not, however, with Mackenzie.

She kissed him with a sweet heat that tempted and teased and drove him quietly out of his mind. Soft. Merciful heavens, her mouth was soft. He wanted to lose himself in her, to carry her to bed and kiss her all over…and forget every painful lesson Carla had taught him about following his heart and trusting a woman.

That thought brought him back to his senses with a jerk, but he still couldn't bring himself to release her. Not yet. Ending the kiss with agonizing slowness, he said hoarsely, "I've got to get out of here while I still can."

"I know," she said huskily. But she still didn't step out of his arms.

"Call me if you need me. I can be here in ten minutes."

"I'll be fine," she assured him. "Stacy and I are going out to dinner. It's girls' night out."

"Then you'd better clean up," he said with a grin and kissed her again. When he finally released her and headed for the stairs, he was whistling and she was weak at the knees.

Standing under the hot rain of the shower ten minutes later, Mackenzie knew she should have been worried. Kissing Patrick was becoming all too easy. He reached for her, wrapped his arms around her, touched her, for heaven's sake, and she completely lost her common sense.

What was she doing?

He was a man who had lost the son he'd thought was his. A son he still obviously adored, she reminded herself. She didn't have to see them together to know that he would be an excellent father…and would, in all likelihood, want more children in the future.

At the thought, the past stirred like slow creeping fog on a dark night. Shivering, Mackenzie hugged herself and couldn't stop the images that rose before her mind's eye, haunting her. Her mother…pregnant, dying. The baby, Mackenzie's little sister—

No! she thought, stiffening as threatening tears stung her eyes. She couldn't go there. She wouldn't! But even as she tried to push the old images away, the hurt that never seemed to completely go away was there, far below the surface…along with a longing she wouldn't even let herself acknowledge.

Quickly turning off the shower, she grabbed a towel. Enough wallowing in self-pity. She refused to indulge herself for longer than five minutes, and then only once every six months. She was good until Easter. She had better things to do.

Stacy would be there in fifteen minutes, she reminded herself. And she knew her too well. She'd take one look at her and know she'd been crying. And Stacy knew there was only one thing Mackenzie ever allowed herself to cry about.

She would deny it, of course, but Stacy wouldn't believe her. She'd worry and that was the last thing she needed right now. The doctor had warned her to watch her blood pressure. She had to avoid stress…

Just thinking about what might happen if Stacy's stress level became too high had Mackenzie quickly drying off, then reaching for her clothes. Within minutes, she was dressed, but drying her hair took longer. It was still slightly damp fifteen minutes later when Stacy arrived.

Hurriedly brushing on mineral makeup, Mackenzie rushed downstairs to let her in and would have sworn she'd completely concealed her earlier tears. When she opened the door to Stacy, however, her friend took one look at her and frowned. "Are you okay?"

"Of course," she said easily, turning away to grab her coat. "I'm just a little tired. It's been a long day. Where do you want to go for dinner? How about something light? Maybe a salad?"

Her gaze still locked on her face, Stacy shrugged. "Whatever. I'm not very hungry. So why was your day so difficult? Is that agent from the Archives still hassling you? What happened with that?"

Mackenzie hadn't told her anything about the break-ins because she hadn't wanted to worry her, and she wasn't about to tell her now. "Agent O'Reilly is still investigating the case," she admitted. "He still doesn't know how Dad ended up with the archival material, but there's some evidence that he wasn't responsible for the thefts."

"Thank God for that! What about the real thief? Has he gotten any leads on that?"

"He's still working on it. Without Dad here to tell us how he ended up with archival documents, it's difficult."

"Is that why you were crying earlier?" she asked smoothly, sliding in the question before Mackenzie could guess her intentions. "You were thinking about your dad?"

"I wasn't crying—"

When Stacy gave her that look, the one that warned Mackenzie she knew her too well to be taken in by any B.S., she gave up in defeat and told her the truth. "Okay, so I got a little emotional. It's no big deal."

Far from satisfied, Stacy frowned. "Emotional? Why? What happened?"

Because of the doctor's orders about stress, Mackenzie hadn't meant to tell her, but she knew better than
anyone how stubborn her friend could be when she
wanted to know something. "Patrick and I have been
spending a lot of time together—"

"Patrick?"

"Agent O'Reilly."

A slow smile curled the corners of her mouth.
"You've been holding out on me. You're dating?"

"No—"

"Oh, Mac, that's wonderful!" Thrilled, she hugged
her fiercely, chattering all the time. "Why didn't you tell
me? Has he kissed you? What's he like? You think this
could be it?"

"No!"

"Don't give me that," she scoffed, grinning. "I know
you. Remember? You wouldn't be giving this guy the
time of day if you didn't really like him—"

"We're not dating," she insisted. "I'm helping him
with the case—"

"And kissing him?" she teased.

Trapped. Stacy had her and they both knew it. Heat
climbing in her cheeks, she sobered. "It's not what
you think. We've been going through the inventory,
looking for more stolen items, and working on a plan
to catch the jackass who took advantage of Dad. The
kisses just happened."

"Yeah, right." Stacy laughed. "Forget about going
out. We can eat something here. I want to hear about
those kisses that 'just happened.'"

* * *

Mackenzie put together a quick meal of cold baked chicken and salad, but Stacy hardly touched it. Instead, she surveyed Mackenzie with the knowing eyes of a friend who went back to the beginning of time with her. "Tell me about Patrick O'Reilly. If you're kissing him, he must be pretty special."

"It was just a kiss, Stace."

"You don't *just kiss* anyone," she said dryly. "Try again."

Stacy knew her too well. Frowning, Mackenzie warned, "Don't make the mistake of thinking there's more to this than there is. I'm not looking for a man."

"I know, and it drives me crazy!" Frustrated, she said, "You've got to quit punishing yourself, Mac. There's no reason why you have to go through life alone."

They'd had this discussion many times before, and Mackenzie's response was always the same. "Men want children. I can't—"

"Yes, you can," she said quickly. "You're just scared. And that's understandable. But your mother's death wasn't your fault."

"I should have been able to save her," she said huskily.

"You were twelve years old, for God's sake! You didn't know anything about delivering babies. And even if you had, you were in the middle of nowhere! There was nothing you could do."

Staring into the fire, Mackenzie looked into the distant past. "Everything would have been different if Dad had been home."

"Not necessarily," Stacy argued. "A blood clot went

to her heart, Mac. Once that happened, she could have been in the hospital with a doctor right there by her side and it wouldn't have mattered. She and the baby still would have died.

"I know you're terrified of having a baby," she added softly. "And justifiably so. But what happened to your mother was a fluke, one of those things that just happened...like a perfect storm. She went into labor early, your dad was out of state at a convention, thinking everything was fine, and you and your mom were alone at your house in the country when an ice storm hit. The phone lines were down, your mom's car didn't have four-wheel drive, and you couldn't get out of the driveway. What are the odds of that happening ever again?"

Mackenzie knew she was right. Logic, however, had nothing to do with fear. "I know you're right, but it doesn't help."

"I just don't want you to pass up something wonderful because you think a man won't want a serious relationship with you if you don't want children. There are other ways to have a baby, including adoption. And who knows? You may change your mind."

When Mackenzie just gave her a pointed look, she said, "It could happen if you'd give yourself a chance. Why don't you go with me to the doctor tomorrow? The doctor wants another sonogram."

Mackenzie's heart jumped at the thought. "Oh, Stace..."

"The baby's fine," Stacy assured her. "*I'm* fine. It's just a routine sonogram and John's not going to be able to go with me. I thought you might want to go and get your first look at your goddaughter."

Her heart squeezing at the thought, she found herself
blinking back tears. "Of course I'll go," she said huskily.
"But you need to know, I'll feel a lot better when Miss
Priss gets here."

Patting her extended stomach, Stacy grinned. "You
and me both."

With Stacy's leave-taking, Mackenzie couldn't
remember the last time she'd felt so alone. Outside, the
wind was on the rise and seemed to take delight in
rattling the windows and making the old building creak
and groan. Chilled to the bone in spite of the fact that
the thermostat was set at a comfortable temperature,
Mackenzie shivered and crowded closer to the fire…
and the images that danced in the flames.

Her mother, urging her to be strong. Stacy, asking her
to go with her to the doctor. Patrick, kissing her, talking
about his son, making her want things she'd never
allowed herself to even consider having. A husband…
family…baby.

Suddenly realizing that she was actually daydream-
ing about a husband and baby, she stiffened, horrified.
What was she doing? That was Stacy's dream, not hers.
She didn't need a husband, didn't need anyone.

And just to prove it to herself, she banked the fire,
set the alarm and strode into the kitchen to make some
brownies. Chocolate made everything better.

Two hours later, when she headed upstairs, the
kitchen and shop were clean, and the emotions of the
day had finally caught up with her. She was emotion-

ally and physically exhausted, and all she wanted to do was fall into bed and not move for the rest of the night.

Sleep, however, didn't come nearly as easily as she'd hoped. Engulfed in silence, she lay there, staring at the dark, listening. For what seemed like an eternity, she heard nothing but the pounding of her heart. Then somewhere, far in the distance, a car alarm suddenly screamed, and two blocks over, a trio of dogs barked sharply in response.

Shivering, Mackenzie pulled the covers higher around her shoulders and told herself there was nothing to be concerned about. Anyone stupid enough to set off a car alarm had already fled. She had nothing to fear.

But five minutes later, just as her heart rate was beginning to return to normal, something scraped against her bedroom window. Just that quickly, fear grabbed her by the throat.

"It's just a tree branch," she whispered in the dark. "Quit being a scaredy-cat. There's nothing to be afraid of."

Logically, she knew that, but her imagination wasn't so sure. Swearing softly, she turned over and punched her pillow. Five minutes, she told herself. If she wasn't asleep in five minutes, she was going to go lie on the couch and turn on the television. There was an all-night marathon of Christmas movies on, and if nothing else, that would distract her from the noises going bump in the night.

Downstairs, out on the street, a car door quietly shut.

Lost in her thoughts, she hardly heard it…then her heart suddenly stopped in mid-beat as the sound registered. Her imagination wasn't playing tricks on her. This time, it wasn't just a tree branch scraping against her window. Someone really was outside.

Was it the thief? Had he come back a third time? She had to call the police, had to—

Down the hall in her father's office, her cell phone rang suddenly, sharply. Startled, she froze. Who would be calling her at midnight?

Suddenly realizing she was lying there, cowering in her bed like a child terrified of the bogeyman, she swore and threw off the covers. She wasn't going to be afraid! she told herself furiously. But as she carefully hurried down the hall in the dark to the office, there was no denying that her legs were anything but steady.

Her ringing phone glowed in the dark on her desk, guiding her straight to it. Snatching it up, she swallowed a sob when she saw Patrick's name on the caller ID.

"Patrick! Thank God!" she cried softly as she flipped open the phone. "I think someone's trying to break in!"

"It's me."

"I know it's you, silly," she hissed, cupping her free hand around her mouth and the phone to keep her voice from possibly carrying to whoever was outside. "I saw your caller ID. Someone's downstairs!"

"It's me," he said again, chuckling. "I'm at the front door. Come down and let me in."

"You're what?"

"I'm downstairs—"

She never remembered hanging up, never remembered running barefoot down the stairs or punching in the code to deactivate the alarm. The next instant, she jerked open the door and threw herself into his arms.

Surprised, he caught her close. "Well, hello. I'm glad to see you, too."

"What are you doing here?" she demanded, pulling back slightly to punch him in the shoulder. "You scared me to death!"

"Sorry." He chuckled, catching her wrist before she could punch him again. "I was concerned about you being here alone. Are you all right?"

"You mean…now that I know no one's breaking in?"

He grinned sheepishly. "Yeah. Sorry about that. I just got to thinking about you and figured you were probably lying awake, staring at the ceiling, worrying about whoever set off your alarm the other night. There are a lot of nutcases out there—"

Her heart still pounding, Mackenzie pressed a quick hand to his mouth. "Don't. I don't want to even think about the nutcases."

Almost immediately, she knew she'd made a mistake. His mouth was soft and oh so seductive. His warm breath caressed her fingers, scrambling her thoughts, making it impossible to think. Dazed, her heart slowly starting to pound, she told herself she was too close, her touch too intimate, stirring memories of kisses better off forgotten. She needed to move, to drop her hand and put some distance between them immediately. But how could she when the very warmth of his breath caressing her fingers seduced her to stay?

He felt it, too—she saw it in his eyes and felt it in the sudden tension that sparked between their bodies. His eyes locked with hers, and for what seemed like an eternity, neither of them seemed to breathe. Then, with infinite care, he wrapped his fingers around her wrist

and slowly, gently, pulled her fingers from his mouth…
and pressed her hand to his heart.

"You're a dangerous woman," he rasped softly. "Do
you know that? I came over here because I couldn't
sleep because of you."

"Me?" she gasped. "What did I do?"

What hadn't she done? he wondered, swallowing a
groan as her fingers shifted slightly under his and unconsciously stroked his chest. She'd taken over his
thoughts, his dreams, and made him wish for things
he'd sworn he'd never let himself want again. He hadn't
meant to like her, hadn't meant to want her, and it was
driving him crazy. *She* was driving him crazy, and there
didn't seem to be a damn thing he could do about it
except quit fighting the pull she had on him and see
where it went. And that scared the hell out of him.

Still, he couldn't stay away from her…which was
really why he'd shown up on her doorstep at midnight.

"I knew you wouldn't tell me if you were scared," he
said gruffly, "so I came over here to check for myself."

"I'm fine," she insisted.

He lifted a dark brow. "Really? So why are you pale
as a ghost?"

"I thought someone was downstairs!"

"Okay, so that's my fault," he admitted gruffly. "I was
afraid you were lying in bed, listening to this old building
moan and groan, and imagining all sorts of things.
Weren't you? C'mon, admit it. You know you were."

Heat climbing in her cheeks, she lifted her chin. "So
what if I was?"

"That's why I'm here," he said simply. "I knew

you'd be scared, and I didn't want you to feel like you had to tough it out all by yourself in the dark. You're not alone, Mac."

Surprise flared in her eyes, then quick, unexpected tears she hurriedly tried to blink away. "How did you know that's how I was feeling?" she asked, stunned.

He'd asked himself the same question as he drove all the way across town at midnight just to check on her. And his answer was always the same. "I don't know," he said simply. "I haven't figured that out yet. I just know I couldn't stay at home and leave you here by yourself when you were feeling so scared. So if it's okay with you, I thought I'd stay awhile and keep you company."

If he'd expected her to give him a fight, he was disappointed. A slow smile curled the corners of her mouth. "TNT is showing Christmas movies all night. I'm game if you are."

"That depends," he retorted, grinning. "Have you got popcorn?"

"Does a leopard have spots?"

"Then we're set to go." He laughed. "Where's the remote?"

Chapter 9

Two hours later, the popcorn had been eaten, Tim Allen had unwittingly become Santa Claus and Mackenzie couldn't seem to keep her eyes open. Totally relaxed and safe with Patrick at her side, her feet propped next to his on the coffee table, she just wanted to snuggle against him and go to sleep.

Instead, she struggled to stay upright and keep her eyes open. But as two-thirty in the morning came and went, she was fighting a losing battle. With a silent sigh, she closed her eyes and gave in to the tug of exhaustion. Within seconds, she was asleep.

Half-asleep himself, Patrick blinked in surprise when she went boneless and slumped against him. "Hey, sleepyhead." He chuckled softly. "Had enough Santa for one night?"

Her only response was a soft, nearly silent, lady-like snore.

Grinning—he couldn't wait to tease her about that later—he slipped his arm around her shoulders, only to remember too late that she was wearing a flannel gown and robe. *Flannel,* he thought with a nearly silent groan as she snuggled against him as naturally as if they'd been lovers for years. He'd always had a weakness for flannel.

She'd probably think he was crazy—most men fantasized about a woman wrapped in something far more seductive...or nothing at all. But there was something about the soft warmth of flannel that he found incredibly appealing. All too easily, he could see his woman alone with him in a cabin in the woods, kissing him as he unbuttoned the buttons of her flannel gown one by one...

Stiffening at the thought, he jerked back to reality to find himself slowly rubbing his hand up and down Mackenzie's arm. Swearing softly, he froze. What the devil was he doing? She wasn't *his* woman! And they sure as hell weren't in a cabin in the woods.

He'd just come over to make sure she was all right and keep her company for a while so she wouldn't be scared, he reminded himself. Obviously, she wasn't scared anymore, so there was no longer any reason for him to stay.

So why are you still here? his conscience growled. *Go home!*

He should have. He was playing with fire and he knew it, but the thought of going home to a cold, empty bed wasn't nearly as appealing as the woman in his arms. And what, after all, would it hurt to hold her a little longer? She was sleeping and he wasn't going to lose his head and take advantage of her, so there was nothing to be worried about.

The matter settled, he eased her closer, stretched his legs out into a more comfortable position and closed his eyes. Almost immediately, Mackenzie's scent swirled around him, teasing his senses, as she turned toward him in her sleep and buried her face against his neck. Just that easily, heat licked along his nerve endings, refusing to be ignored.

Swallowing a curse, he silently ordered himself to think about something else, anything but the soft, sleeping woman in his arms. He was, however, fighting a losing battle. His senses were attuned to very breath, every sigh, every sweet, sleepy movement of her body.

Right then and there, he should have kissed her good-night and got the hell out of there. But even when the woman was dead to the world in his arms, he knew he couldn't walk away from her. Right or wrong, he wasn't going anywhere.

They couldn't, however, sleep on the couch for the rest of the night without both of them ending up at a chiropractor in the morning. With a murmur that was her name, he gently eased away from her, but only to reach for her again as he came to his feet.

Stirring, she frowned in confusion as her eyes fluttered open. "Patrick? What—"

"The movie's over," he said gruffly. "I'm just carrying you to bed."

Too tired to protest, she leaned her head against his

shoulder and slipped her arms around his neck. "I'm sorry," she said, yawning. "I can't seem to stay awake."

Tightening his arms around her, he carried her into her bedroom and leaned over to gently deposit her in her bed. "Go back to sleep," he said quietly, kissing her on the cheek. "I'm going to turn off the lights in the living room."

Surprised, she reached for him, catching his hand before he could step away from the bed. "You're not leaving, are you?"

In the light that streamed into the bedroom from the living room, his eyes met hers. "Do you want me to?"

They both knew what he was asking. If he stayed, he would be sharing her bed. It was that simple...and that complicated. Later, they would have to deal with the ramifications of that, but for now, it all came down to a one-word answer.

Her fingers tightened around his. "No," she said huskily. "Stay."

When she looked up at him with need in her eyes, the world could have tilted on its axis and completely lost its way in the universe and he wouldn't had noticed or cared. "I'll be right back," he promised, and strode into the living room to turn off the lights and TV.

He was back almost immediately, only taking time to pull off his boots, before he was sliding into bed next to her, clothes and all. Surprised, Mackenzie laughed as he pulled her into his arms. "You've still got your clothes on."

"So do you." He chuckled. "We'll deal with that later."

Her heart pounding, she expected him to kiss her

senseless, but she quickly discovered that he wasn't a man who did the expected. Lying on his side with her in his arms, he reached for her hand and pulled it to his mouth to press a slow, lingering kiss to her pulse. In the time it took to draw in a sharp breath, she was throbbing.

"Patrick…"

All his attention on the warm, sensitive skin of her wrist, he smiled. "Hmm?"

She couldn't summon a single word other than his name. Then he teased her racing pulse with his tongue, and her senses scattered. Dazed, she leaned into him, breathless, aching. How could he stir need in her so effortlessly when he'd barely touched her?

Too late, she realized this was all a mistake. She was too susceptible where he was concerned, too vulnerable. From the moment she'd met him, he'd caught her heart off guard and made her want things she couldn't have. She should have thanked him for checking on her and helping her get through the worst of the evening, then walked him to the door and told him good-night. It would have been the smart thing to do. The safe thing to do.

But she was so tired of playing it safe, of protecting her heart, of running from hurt, and in the process, denying herself the sweet, breath-catching touch of a man. Especially this man. The scent and heat of his lean, hard length next to her tangled her thoughts and called to her in the dark, filling her with longing. Just this once, couldn't she give in to that need? Just this once, couldn't she forget the past, if only for a little while, and be like any other woman who found herself unbearably drawn to a man she couldn't stop thinking of? Dreaming of? Just this once, couldn't she...

His warm breath teasing her, distracting her, tempting her, he kissed her wrist again, then slowly trailed soft, butterfly kisses up her arm to the inside of her elbow. She moaned and blindly reached for him. Just that easily, the decision was made.

His mouth, hot and hungry, found hers in the dark and slowly, effortlessly seduced. Her mind blurred. When his hands moved to the tie belt of her robe, she couldn't think of a single reason to object. Intoxicated, aching to the depth of her being, she sank into him and closed her eyes on a sigh, lost to everything but the taste of him.

Sweet. How could he have known she was so sweet? he wondered with a dazed groan. It seemed like he'd been wanting her like this from the moment he'd first laid eyes on her, and nothing he'd imagined alone in his bed in the dark of the night in any way matched reality. She was a witch, a seductress, with the touch of an angel.

Her fingers brushed over him, and every nerve ending in his body jumped in response. In the span of seconds, all he could think of was how much he wanted her...now!

"Enough!" he growled, and trapped her hand between their bodies.

He felt her smile against him, her warm breath a rush against his hot skin, and wanted nothing more than to draw out the pleasure until they were both mindless with need. But as their clothes disappeared piece by piece in the dark, intimate shadows that engulfed them and he committed every inch of her to memory, she threatened his control in a thousand different ways.

It was her scent—it drove him wild, he decided, only to change his mind almost immediately. No, it was the incredible softness of her skin—he couldn't seem to stop touching her. He gathered her closer, then closer still, and groaned as her bare legs tangled with his, skin against skin. Then her hands moved over him, caressing, stroking, and closed around him. Need, sharp and swift, clawed at him in the darkness of the night.

Kissing her fiercely, desperately, he just barely remembered to protect them both before she was reaching for him, pulling him down to her, into her. And when he tasted her surprise on her tongue, he realized the last thing she'd expected was the emotions that swamped her from all angles. Bewildered, stunned, she kissed him like a woman who had been alone too long, hurt too much, and hadn't realized until now that she needed this time with him a thousand times more than she'd allowed herself to admit.

Tenderness washed over him. Who was this woman who was such a constant surprise to him? Questions tugged at him, but then she moved with him, the tantalizing feel of her body under him, surrounding him, seducing him and stealing his thoughts. Pleasure, sweet and pure and breath-stealing, came rushing at him like a freight train.

A groan ripping from his throat, he struggled for the last shreds of his control, but then Mackenzie arched under him, her cry of delight shattering the night. In the span of a heartbeat, he was lost to everything but the sweet, hot, intense satisfaction that washed over him, dragging him under.

* * *

Nothing had ever felt so right.

Long after Patrick had gathered her close and fallen asleep with her in his arms, Mackenzie lay there with her head on his naked chest, listening to the beat of his heart, reeling. What had he done to her? she wondered, stricken. This wasn't supposed to happen. She wasn't supposed to feel like she'd just made love with her soul mate for the first time in what felt like a thousand years.

She didn't believe in soul mates, she told herself, shaken. She couldn't. She couldn't let herself consider even for a second that there was someone she could love, someone who would love her and accept her fears from the past and the promises she'd made to herself ages ago.

Because even if that was possible, that man would never be Patrick.

Pain squeezed her heart at the thought. After everything his ex-wife had done, she didn't blame him for thinking he would never trust a woman again. But with time, she knew he would get past the hurt and step back into life. With time, he would learn to trust again... and fall in love. And with time, he would become a father again.

All too easily, she could see him with a child...a little boy with dark, curly hair and mischief dancing in his green eyes whom he could teach to play ball and ride a bike and fish and hunt. Or a daughter, she thought, longing filling her eyes with tears, who would adore him and wrap him around her little finger with just a flash of her cute little dimples. She could see them together now, her smile melting his heart as she climbed into his lap with her favorite book, her arms circling his neck when he tucked her in and kissed her good-night…

Suddenly realizing how she was torturing herself, she should have slipped out of his arms and spent what was left of the night working or addressing Christmas cards or anything that distracted her from the man in her bed. But how could she when this would be the only night she would ever have with him? How could she deny herself that?

So as the hours slipped by one by one and dawn drew closer, then closer still, she tried to pretend that time was a concept that had outlived its usefulness. There was no yesterday, no tomorrow, no past, no future. All she had was now, today…and Patrick.

In the weak moonlight that filtered through the window and spilled across the bed, she studied him, fascinated. It had been so long since she'd shared her bed with a man—she'd forgotten how…warm…the male of the species was. It was like sleeping with a blast furnace, she thought. How was she ever going to be able to sleep in her bed again without thinking of him?

Stricken, she quickly swallowed a sob. She wasn't, she realized, going to be able to sleep with him the rest of the night. Not when she was torturing herself with thoughts of what might have been. Quickly slipping out from under the covers, she found her robe in the darkness and rushed out before she made a complete fool of herself. Tears blinding her, she never saw Patrick reach for her in his sleep.

* * *

The first faint light of morning was brightening the eastern horizon when Patrick stepped into the kitchen. In the process of pouring herself a cup of coffee, Mackenzie looked up and felt her heart stop. After she'd left him sleeping in her bed, she'd spent what was left of the night tackling her Christmas card list and getting her emotions under control. When she'd heard him stirring upstairs and her heart hadn't even skipped a beat, she'd have sworn she could look him right in the eye without the loving they'd shared last night being right there between them.

She'd couldn't have been more wrong. The second her eyes met his, her heart remembered…everything. She could feel his touch, taste his kiss, hear the thunder of his heart.

"Good morning," he said gruffly.

Heat climbing her cheeks, she quickly reached for a spare mug in the cabinet and poured him a cup of coffee. "Good morning. I was just about to start breakfast. Are you hungry?" she asked brightly as she carefully handed him the mug.

"I can't stay," he said regretfully. "I don't even really have time for coffee. I've got to be in court this morning at eight to testify against an idiot who saw *National Treasure* and wanted to see if there really was a map on the back of the Declaration of Independence."

"Are you serious? Who would be that stupid?"

"An MIT graduate," he retorted in disgust. "Talk about a moron. He thought he'd figured out the security code and gave it a shot."

Her lips twitched. "Obviously, he wasn't as smart as he thought he was."

"Oh, he cracked the code to get in the building," he admitted, "but all that got him was five steps inside the door before sensors went off and set off alarms all over the building. He was in lockdown before he could even think about running."

"And what did he think he was going to do with the Declaration of Independence when he got his hands on it? Sell it on eBay?"

Grinning, he shot her a pointed look. "Why not? eBay worked for you."

He had her and they both knew it. "Okay." She chuckled. "Guilty as charged. But I didn't know what I was selling was hot. And it wasn't the Declaration of Independence!"

"True." Glancing at his watch, he swore softly. "I've got to get going or I'm going to be late." But when he set his coffee mug down on the countertop, he didn't leave as she'd expected. Instead, he eliminated the distance between them with a single step and took her hand. "Can I take a rain check on breakfast?" he asked huskily.

She should have said no. She'd already made the decision that he was one of those intoxicating, addictively wonderful mistakes that she wasn't going to repeat. And breakfast, of all meals, was the one she had no business giving him a rain check on. Breakfast meant...dinner the night before...long, sensuous kisses as they made their way to her bed...waking up wrapped in each other's arms and making love again with knowing hands and clever mouths and tongues—

"Mackenzie? Sweetheart, I don't know what I said, but I'm never going to make my court date if you don't stop looking at me like that. Where are you?"

His teasing tone snapped her back to attention as nothing else could. Her cheeks suddenly hot with color, she blinked and found him watching her with a broad grin. "No," she said hoarsely. "No rain checks."

"No?" He chuckled. "If I had five minutes, I bet I could change your mind on that."

"I bet you could, too." She laughed. "But then you'd be late to court. Are you willing to risk that?"

Not a man to pass up a challenge, he chuckled and leaned down to drop a quick, hungry kiss on her mouth. She was still floating when he laughed and walked out.

Mackenzie didn't know how she got through the morning and early afternoon. There was plenty of work to do, but she'd had practically no sleep the previous night, and it was catching up with her. By eleven, her eyes were starting to glaze over. By one, she was nodding off and misfiling receipts.

Irritated with herself, she was seriously considering closing the shop for a couple of hours so she could go upstairs and take a nap. Then the front door opened and the John Philip Sousa boomed a welcome.

Surprised—she hadn't had a customer all day—she looked up, only to gasp as Stacy walked in with her stomach leading the way. "Oh, my God, your doctor's appointment!"

"You forgot?"

She winced at her stricken look. "I'm sorry! With

everything that's been going on, it just slipped my mind. But I can still go with you," she assured her. "Just give me a second to get my purse and coat. I'll be right back."

"What do you mean…'with everything that's been going on'?" Stacy called after her. "Does *everything* have anything to do with that good-looking hunk you're dating?"

"I'm not—"

"Yes, you are. You've got that look."

Horrified, Mackenzie rushed into her bedroom and examined herself in her dresser mirror. She couldn't have *that* look! Stacy was just imagining things. She wanted everyone to be married and sappy in love. She'd have said the same thing if she'd been crying her eyes out.

Quickly pulling on her coat, she hurried back down the stairs, silently cursing the blush that singed her cheeks when Stacy grinned. "I like him," she told her. "Okay? That's all it is."

Grinning, Stacy said, "Mmm-hmm. And when we were in middle school, I liked Earnest Rucker, too. But you couldn't have paid me enough to kiss him. What time did lover boy leave this morning?"

"Seven—" Suddenly realizing what she'd just admitted, she couldn't help but laugh. "You're outrageous."

Stacy's brown eyes twinkled with triumph. "But good. You've gotta admit I'm good, Mac."

"Yes, you are." She laughed. "And you're going to be late if we don't get out of here."

"We've got time," she said with a dismissive wave

of her hand. "First I want to hear about Mr. Wonderful. Is this serious?"

Mackenzie would have given anything to say yes. Instead, all she could say was, "Nothing's changed, Stacy, so don't start planning the wedding because it's not going to happen."

"You don't know that," she argued as Mackenzie taped a note to the door announcing she was closing the shop early, set the alarm, then hurried outside with her. "You should give him a chance. For all you know, he doesn't even want children. Not everyone does, you know."

All too easily, Mackenzie could see Patrick's face as he'd talked about his son. "No, there's no question he wants children," she said as she climbed into the passenger seat of Stacy's Camry, which was parked at the curb.

When she told her about his ex-wife and the son he'd lost who wasn't his, Stacy gasped, horrified. "What a horrible woman! She lies to him their entire marriage, then decides to tell him the truth when she files for divorce? How many years did it take her to develop a conscience?"

"Three," Mackenzie said with a grimace as Stacy pulled away from the curb and jumped into the traffic.

"Three! That poor little boy! If she cared anything at all about him, she would have kept her mouth shut and let him have the only father he'd ever known."

"Can you imagine what it must feel like to lose a child that way?" Mackenzie said. "He's still walking and talking and breathing, but he will never be Patrick's son again."

Her hand moving from the steering wheel to her

very pregnant stomach and the baby that rested just under her heart, Stacy paled at the thought. "No. It must be an ongoing nightmare that haunts him every day. It would me."

"And if you lost a child that way," Mackenzie told her quietly, "wouldn't you want children again? Once you let yourself trust again, wouldn't you want your own child?"

"*I* would," she agreed. "But that doesn't mean Patrick feels the same way. After everything he's been through, he may decide he doesn't want to risk that kind of heartache again."

"But he may not."

"True," she agreed, "but that's something you'll have to discuss with him at some point in the future. You don't have to decide anything right now."

Mackenzie desperately wished she had the luxury of time, but she didn't. Not when she had no defenses when it came to Patrick. She couldn't put her heart on the line for what-ifs—or put Patrick's at risk because he made her ache for what might have been. "I can't wait that long," she said huskily.

Tears misting her eyes, Stacy reached over to squeeze her hand. "Give yourself some time and just enjoy his company for a while, Mac. Everything will work out the way it's supposed to."

"Maybe."

"No maybe," she said with a smile, squeezing her hand one last time as she pulled into the parking lot of the medical building where her gynecologist's office was located. "Look at me. Everyone told me I'd never be able to have a baby because of all the problems I had when I was teenager, and look? Less than six weeks from now, little Miss Savannah Green will be waltzing into our world and taking over."

Mackenzie grinned. "And you're going to spoil her rotten."

"Just a little." She laughed. "Just when she smiles and cries and—"

"Breathes." Mackenzie chuckled. "I can see it now. She's going to run you and John ragged."

Far from concerned, Stacy beamed. "I know. Isn't it wonderful? C'mon, let's go check her out."

Chapter 10

Mackenzie followed Stacy and the nurse into the examining room and was caught off guard when she felt a kick of nerves in her stomach. There was, she told herself, absolutely nothing to be worried about. Dr. Decker had ordered sonograms at regular intervals to make sure there were no surprises with the baby, so this exam was just routine. If everything looked all right—and there was no reason to believe that it wouldn't—she and Stacy would be able to make it to Fritzbee's in time for the lunch special they both loved.

But when the nurse helped Stacy change, then get up on the examining table, fear from the past rose up before Mackenzie like a ghost, setting her heart pounding. Suddenly, there didn't seem to be quite enough air in the room…or starch in her legs. Shaken, she sank into the nearest chair.

Dr. Decker was an attractive older man with a quick smile and twinkle in his eyes, who had the reassuring presence of a kindly grandfather. When he walked in, he greeted Stacy with an affectionate smile and a pat on the hand, only to frown when he noticed Mackenzie and her pale face. "Are you all right?"

Struggling for control, Mackenzie nodded. "It's just nerves," she admitted huskily. "I'll be fine. Just give me a minute."

"This is my best friend, Mackenzie Sloan," Stacy told the doctor quickly. "I told you about her. She's going to be the baby's godmother."

"Oh, yes," he said, remembering, shaking hands with Mackenzie. "It's nice to meet you. Stacy said you were worried about her and the baby."

Tears welling in her eyes, she nodded. "I don't know if she told you about my mother."

Squeezing her hand, he smiled, understanding. "Yes, she did, but this isn't the same situation at all. She's in excellent health except for her blood pressure, and we're keeping a close eye on that. I see her every week, she's sticking to her diet and resting. She and the baby are both going to be fine."

"See," Stacy told her, pleased. "I told you there was nothing to worry about. Just wait. Six weeks from now, we'll both get to hold her. She's going to be beautiful, Mac."

She was so excited, Mackenzie couldn't help but

feel guilty for dampening her joy in any way. "I'm sorry. I'll try not to worry."

"Good," Dr. Decker said. "Now let's get a picture of the little princess and see how she's grown."

As the nurse prepared Stacy for the sonogram, Mackenzie moved to her side and took the hand Stacy held out to her. Then, seconds later, Dr. Decker slid the sonogram sensor over Stacy's extended belly, and suddenly, there was the baby's grainy image on the monitor.

Stacy laughed in delight, but Mackenzie hardly heard her. From the moment she'd told Stacy she would go with her to the doctor, she'd known this moment would come, the moment when she found herself dealing with the reality of not just Stacy's pregnancy, but the fact that that was a very real baby she was carrying and would soon give birth to.

She'd thought she was prepared. That she would see the sonogram image and be able to emotionally distance herself from the reality of what it really was. But as her eyes locked on the surprisingly clear picture of tiny fingers and toes, rounded bottom and sweet, pert nose, she suddenly found herself fighting tears and a longing that came from her very soul.

Too late, she realized she never should have agreed to accompany Stacy today. Not for this. She could have come up with an excuse—she couldn't afford to close the shop, she had a doctor's appointment herself, she didn't feel well. Stacy would have understood…

And seen right through her, she silently acknowledged. It didn't matter. She couldn't stand this. She wasn't supposed to feel this ache, this need that burned in her heart like a hot flame. She couldn't bear it. She had to get out of there.

Her only thought to get away, she didn't realize her tortured thoughts were right there on her face for anyone to see until Stacy's hand tightened around hers. Her gaze flew to hers, and the understanding she saw in her friend's eyes was almost her undoing. "I'm sorry." She sniffed, wiping impatiently at the tears that spilled over her lashes. "I don't know what's wrong with me. I didn't expect—"

"I didn't, either," Stacy admitted, tears misting her own eyes. "John was able to come with me for the first sonogram and we both cried like babies."

"But it's your baby."

"You're her godmother—she's going to be your baby, too," she promised. "Everything's going to be all right, Mac. You'll see. Everything's finally going to be all right."

She sounded so sure. And Mackenzie had never wanted to believe something so badly in her life. Her gaze drifting back to the screen, she felt hope stir in her heart for the first time in a long, long time. Maybe...

Patrick liked to think he was a man with a hell of a lot of common sense. A pragmatic man who wasn't ruled by his emotions, but rather by reason and logic. Whether he was dealing with a case at work or life in general, he analyzed the facts, came to a conclusion and developed a strategy that would help him achieve his objectives. One plus one equaled two. End of story.

Except when it came to Mackenzie.

Trying to focus on the final report he had to write on

the theft of Lincoln's handwritten notes of the Gettysburg Address and the conviction of the two thieves who had stolen the documents when they were on loan from the Lincoln Library to Georgetown University, he swore softly as his thoughts were pulled back again and again to last night…and Mackenzie. It had been hours since he'd left her that morning, and he could still smell her scent on his skin, still taste her on his tongue—

Abruptly realizing where his thoughts had wandered, he swore softly and tried to jerk his attention back to work, but he was fighting a losing battle. And he had no one to blame but himself. He never should have made love to her.

Images teased him…Mackenzie…her quick smile lighting her eyes, the tempting softness of her skin, her mouth moving under his with a tender hunger that haunted his dreams. She only had to touch him, sigh his name, to make him forget the past and why he'd sworn to never let a woman get to him again.

If he'd had any sense, he would have turned the case over to the FBI and let someone else handle it…and Mackenzie. But even though he knew it was the safe thing to do, he knew it was already too late for that. He wasn't turning her or her case over to anyone.

His office phone rang, jerking him back to his surroundings. Scowling at the unfinished report still on his computer screen, he reached absently for the phone. "Agent O'Reilly."

"Patrick?"

Immediately recognizing his ex-wife's voice, he stiffened. After their divorce, when she'd made it clear that Tommy was lost to him and she never wanted to hear from him again, he'd respected her wishes. He hadn't called her, hadn't driven down the street where she and Tommy lived, had even steered clear of friends they both shared. He done every damn thing she asked because he'd known a quick, clean break was best for everyone concerned. But what the hell was he supposed to do when she was the one calling him?

"Is Tommy all right?"

"He's fine," Carla quickly assured him. "He's on a field trip to the zoo today. He was so excited, I could hardly get him to sit still long enough to eat breakfast this morning."

All too easily, he could see Tommy, his blue eyes bright with anticipation as he forced down his favorite breakfast of pancakes and sausage. The second Carla gave the nod of approval, he would have been out the door like a shot, beating her to the car by at least five minutes, where he'd have waited impatiently for her to join him.

C'mon, Mom! We gotta go. Miss Becky said not to be late.

Patrick could hear him as clearly as if he stood right there in his office, shifting from foot to foot, barely able to contain his impatience to be gone. And it hurt, dammit. He'd lost two years with his son...two birthdays, two Christmases he would never get back...while he tried to accept the fact that not only was his son not his son, but that he would never be a part of his life again. It hadn't been easy, but he'd managed to bring the hurt under control. Or at least, he'd thought he had.

Then Tommy called and asked for a ride to school. So much for progress.

A muscle ticking in his jaw, he growled, "What do you want, Carla? I'm busy."

Even to his own ears, his tone was harsh, and with good reason. She was up to something, and he wasn't, by God, going to let her get away with hurting him a second time. The sooner she knew that, the better.

Half expecting her to snap back at him, he was caught off guard when she said quietly, "We need to talk."

"Yeah, right," he snorted. "You did all your talking in court and got everything you wanted. From where I'm standing, there's nothing left to say."

For a moment, he thought she'd hung up. Then she sighed tiredly. "I don't want to fight, Patrick. I just need to talk to you. It's about Tommy—"

"You said he was fine!"

"He is. It's just…"

"What?" he demanded. "What is this about, Carla? Just spit it out. I'm not in the mood for games."

"This isn't a game," she retorted, stung. "I just need to talk to you and I don't want to do it over the phone. It'll take all of five minutes."

He heard the tears in her voice and frowned. There'd been a time when he'd hated the idea of her crying and would have done anything to make her smile again. But not now, he realized, stunned. He felt nothing. He was no longer responsible for her happiness.

"Well?" she asked. "Can you give me five minutes or not?"

Still reeling, he hardly heard her impatient tone. He

didn't love her, didn't want her, and only considered giving in to her demands because of Tommy. "I'll meet you at the café in an hour," he said coolly. "If that won't work for you, then we'll have to do this tomorrow. I'm booked all day today."

"I'll be there," she promised, and quietly hung up.

The Atrium Café was located directly across the street from the National Archives. In the summer, it was always packed with tourists, who usually collected around the large fountain in the nearby National Sculpture Garden, where they could rest in the shade of cherry trees and enjoy the musical ballet that played continuously throughout the day. The fountain was quiet now, however, the patio tables and chairs that offered alfresco dining put away for the winter.

Inside, however, the café was a beehive of activity. It was barely eleven and early for lunch, but local government employees and tourists were already in line at the café's cafeteria-style counter, and the dining room was quickly filling up.

In spite of that, Patrick spotted Carla immediately. Seated by a window that overlooked the fountain, she had already ordered coffee for both of them and was sipping hers as she stared solemnly out the window.

Taking a moment to study her unobserved, he frowned. In the two years since their divorce, she'd lost weight. And if the expression on her face was anything to go by, she hadn't found the happiness she'd thought she would when she walked away from him and their marriage. She looked older, more pensive, disillusioned.

He still, however, didn't trust her.

Crossing to her, he approached her warily. "Good morning," he said gruffly.

Startled, her eyes flew to his. "Patrick! I didn't see you come in."

"You looked a million miles away," he said as he pulled out the chair opposite her.

She shrugged, her weak smile little more than a grimace as she handed him the coffee she'd ordered for him. "Not miles. Years. I've been doing a lot of thinking lately."

Regret—her voice was heavy with it, her eyes misted with it. Sitting back in his chair, Patrick said quietly, "Looking back won't change anything. What's done is done. We can't go back. So if that's what this is about—"

"No!" she said quickly when he set down his coffee and moved as if to rise from his chair. "Some things can be changed. If you'll just listen."

"Not us, Carla," he said flatly. "That's done for good."

Tears welled in her eyes, but she quickly blinked them away. "I know. And that's totally and completely my fault. Our marriage was based on a lie. My lie. And I don't ever expect you to forgive me for that. That's not why I wanted to talk to you."

When she hesitated, he said, "I wasn't lying when I told you I only have a few minutes, Carla. I'm not trying to rush you, but…"

"I know. Sorry." Straightening her shoulders, she met his gaze head-on. "I made a terrible mistake when I refused to let you see Tommy anymore. It was selfish and spiteful of me, but I wasn't thinking clearly at the time.

All I can say in my own defense is that I thought a clean break would be best for everyone, especially if Tommy was ever going to have a relationship with Wayne.

"I know," she said when fury flashed in his eyes at the mention of Tommy's biological father. "I cut you out of his life for a man who never had any interest in being his father. You were the one he loved, the one who was always there for him, right from the beginning, the one he wants to be like. I hurt you both terribly. Saying I'm sorry doesn't begin to express how much I regret that."

Tears streamed down her face, and there was no question that she meant every word. There was, however, nothing Patrick could say that would take away the pain tearing at her. She had to live with the choices she'd made in life. They all did.

"You did what you thought you had to do," he said quietly. "I don't know what else you want me to say—"

"I want you to see Tommy again," she blurted out. "To be his father, to share visitation with me the same way you would have if he was your biological son."

She couldn't have shocked Patrick more if she'd reached across the table and stabbed him in the heart. What kind of idiot did she think he was? Did she really think he'd fall for her apology and sad tale of regret and let her dangle Tommy before him like a carrot she could snatch away whenever the mood struck her?

Livid, he snapped, "How stupid do you think I am? This meeting is over." And not giving her a chance to say another word, he pushed to his feet and walked out.

"Patrick! Dammit, will you wait? Why are you so angry? I thought you would want this!"

"Want this?" he echoed furiously, whirling on her as she rushed after him and followed him outside. "You think I would want to give you the power to hurt me again, to yank my son away from me whenever you got a bee in your bonnet? Sorry. Been there, done that. I'm never letting you jerk my chain again."

Fuming, he left her standing there and headed for the Archives. This time, she didn't follow him. *Good,* he thought furiously. If she dared to call him again, he'd change his damn number. Let her find some other poor fool to torture—

"I'll put it in writing and file it with the courts."

Her words carried on the cold breeze that whipped down the National Mall and caught up with him just as he was about to cross the street to the Archives. *Ignore her,* he told himself. *Keep walking.*

"Your lawyer can draw up the papers."

There were a lot of things he could walk away from, but his son wasn't one of them. Turning, he found her twenty yards away, huddled in her jacket, the wind whipping her black hair in her eyes as she met his gaze.

"Why?" he asked hoarsely. "Why are you doing this? What do you want?"

"I told you. I want you to be Tommy's father again. His full, legal father, with all the rights of a father."

"Why? Why now? What the hell's going on?"

"He needs you," she said simply. "He's been very unhappy since the divorce. He hasn't been sleeping well—he's having nightmares and has to sleep with a light on. His teacher says he's falling asleep in class and having problems with some of the other boys on the playground. He came home with a split lip yesterday. He got in a fight with an older boy.

"He needs you, Patrick. He needs both of us. Not together," she said quickly when he stiffened. "This isn't a trick to get you back. This is strictly about Tommy having two parents who love him and will work together to give him the security he needs to be a happy little boy again."

Studying her with eyes that missed little, Patrick hesitated, torn between anger and a hope he didn't want to put a name to. Was she serious? She knew that regardless of what she or a judge or any DNA tests said, he was and always would be Tommy's father. He would do anything for him. Carla was another matter.

Could he trust her to keep her word? She'd made promises in the past, all based on lies. Was this another one of those promises?

"If I agree to this, it's for life," he warned. "I don't care who you get involved with or marry, if you get mad at me or anyone I get involved with—it doesn't matter. Our agreement stands. There will be no fighting between us on anything concerning Tommy. If we don't agree on something, we keep talking until we get it hashed out. You're his mother and I'm his father, and there will be nothing but respect between us. Understood?"

She nodded, tears glistening in her eyes. "Understood."

"I'll have my lawyer draw up the paperwork," he said gruffly, "then send it to your lawyer for his approval."

"That's not necessary."

"Oh, yes, it is," he said flatly. "If this blows up in my face and ends up in court, your lawyer's not going to

be able to claim you didn't have legal representation."
The matter settled, he said, "I've got to go. I'll call
Tommy tonight, if that's okay with you."

"I know he'll love that," she said huskily. "Thank
you, Patrick."

He wasn't doing it for her and they both knew it. "I've
got to get back to work." Without another word, he turned
and crossed the street to the Archives and was lucky he
didn't get hit by a truck. Was he really getting his son back?

Long after she returned to her shop, Mackenzie was
still in a daze. With a will of their own, her thoughts kept
drifting back to Stacy and the sonogram of the baby…
and yearnings she'd been suppressing for years, refusing even to acknowledge.

Shaken, she stiffened. No! She wouldn't do this! she
told herself fiercely. She wouldn't torture herself with
dreams of babies, of a husband and family of her own,
of a world of stuffed toys and puppy dogs and the tooth
fairy. Santa and the Easter bunny were never coming to
her house, and the only trick-or-treaters who came to
her door would always belong to someone else. She
knew that. Accepted it.

Or at least, she always had in the past.

And it was the sudden doubts, the tantalizing what-
ifs, that were tearing her apart. She'd always had control
of her emotions, always known what she wanted—and
couldn't risk. The fact that Stacy was having a baby
shouldn't have anything to do with her and the decision
she's made when she wasn't even old enough to drive.
She had to stop this!

Forcing herself to focus, she settled at the computer to enter the day's business in QuickBooks, then read her e-mails. Despite his fascination with the past, her father had been smart enough to recognize the importance of the Internet to a small business. He'd had a Web site since the mid-'90s and, consequently, had customers and friends all over the world. Keeping up with that end of the business was one of her favorite parts of her day.

Smiling as she read an e-mail from one of her father's oldest friends, who was looking for some of Thomas Jefferson's architectural drawings of Monticello, she sent him a quick reply, informing him she didn't currently have anything of Jefferson's, but she would contact some other dealers and see what she could find.

Immediately sending out an e-mail to her cohorts for the architectural drawings and some other items she'd had requests for, she then moved on to the next e-mail, then the next. There were orders for three rare books, a two-hundred-year-old map of Canada and a complete first-edition set of Mark Twain's work.

She'd package them tonight and get them in the mail tomorrow, she thought as she clicked on the next e-mail. She'd make a quick trip to the post office at lunch—

Her heart stopped in her breast as her gaze skimmed the e-mail she'd just opened:

Dear Ms. Sloan, I'm writing in response to your ad in The Patriot *regarding the handwritten copy of FDR's address to the nation after the Japanese attack on Pearl Harbor. I would like to discuss the item with you and examine it, if possible. You can reach me at lionhunter27@dctc.com. I look forward to hearing from you soon.*

Sincerely,

Hunter Lyons

The roar of her blood loud in her ears, Mackenzie reached for her phone and punched in Patrick's number. The second he answered, she said, "Someone responded to the ad in *The Patriot*."

Chapter 11

Standing behind Mackenzie, who sat at her computer, Patrick read over her shoulder as she brought up the e-mail she'd received in response to her ad. "Hunter Lyons, huh?" he snorted. "It's probably an alias. Let's check Google."

Mackenzie quickly typed in the name and whistled in surprise when Hunter Lyons, author and history professor at Boston College, popped up. "Wow. He's got quite an impressive résumé."

"Hunter Lyons does. I'm not sure Professor Lyons is the one who really answered the ad."

Surprised, Mackenzie frowned. "You think someone stole his identity?"

He shrugged. "It's possible. See if you can find a phone number for him."

Within minutes, Mackenzie had a number for an H. Lyons in Concord, Massachusetts. Reaching for the phone, Patrick quickly punched in the number, then hit the speaker button so Mackenzie could hear the call.

Three rings later, a deep male voice answered. "Hunter Lyons."

Introducing himself as an agent with the Office of the Inspector General for the National Archives, Patrick added, "I'm currently investigating several thefts from the Archives, Professor, and was wondering if you could answer some questions for me."

Surprised, he said, "Is there a problem, Agent O'Reilly?"

"That's what I'm trying to discover, sir. I intercepted an e-mail concerning the sale of a historical document advertised in *The Patriot*. Did you respond in any way to that ad, sir?"

The other man didn't hesitate. "I haven't bought any historical documents in several years, Agent O'Reilly, and those were purchased through a broker. Why would you think I had?"

"Because whoever answered the ad used your name," he said simply.

"What?"

"Would you verify your e-mail address for me, sir?"

"Lyonprof1 at AOL," he answered promptly, without hesitation.

Not surprised, Patrick said, "I'm trying to figure out how your name came into this. Naturally, your students and coworkers at Boston College know who you are, but all the evidence points to the fact that whoever stole these documents from the Archives is from the D.C. area. Do you know anyone in Washington who might use your name to buy stolen documents?"

"I don't count thieves among my acquaintances, Agent O'Reilly," he said flatly. "Whoever did this certainly isn't someone I know, though there's a logical explanation of how he came up with my name. I wrote an article for *Smithsonian* magazine that was published last week."

Patrick exchanged a speaking glance with Mackenzie. "That may be the explanation we're looking for, Professor Lyons. Thank you for your help."

"I don't know that I did that much," he said honestly, "but I'd appreciate it if you'd let me know how this turns out. Knowing someone is out there using my name to perpetuate a crime is more than a little disconcerting."

"I'll keep you posted," Patrick assured him. "Thanks again for your help."

"Now what?" Mackenzie asked the second he hung up.

"We set a trap and set up a meeting."

"But we don't even know for sure that whoever answered the ad is really the person we're looking for," she argued. "Just because he used an alias doesn't mean he's a thief—he may just want anonymity. That's not that unusual, especially when the buyer is making a major purchase. And the real thief might not have even seen the ad."

He knew she was playing devil's advocate, but every instinct he had told him they were on the right track. "You and I both know collectors check all the Web sites, including *The Patriot*'s, for the latest treasures. If the thief is raking in the dough dealing in stolen documents, trust me, he's online every day, keeping up on what's out there and what it's selling for."

"But how can you be sure *he's* the one? He could be a legitimate collector who doesn't like to give out his real name to just anyone who posts an ad."

"True," he agreed. "But whoever walked out of the Archives with the stolen documents broke in here and stole the receipts that probably identified him, then came back a second time, obviously to retrieve the stolen material. Since that didn't work, he's got to find another way to get his hands on as much of the incriminating evidence against him as possible. If he has to, he'll buy it under an alias and assume no one will ever know the difference."

"And if we meet with this guy and he's not the real thief, then what?"

"No harm, no foul," he said with a shrug. "*If* he checks out. Write him back and tell him you'll meet him tomorrow at the Theodore Roosevelt Memorial at ten in the morning. And he needs to bring cash," he added.

In the process of writing the e-mail, she looked up at him in surprise. "That's awfully secluded."

Patrick could understand her concern. The T.R. memorial was on an island directly across the Potomac from the Kennedy Center. It had been chosen as the site for Roosevelt's memorial because of his stand on conservation and love of nature, and it was well off the beaten path. Visitors parked in the parking area, then had to walk down a winding path to reach the memorial itself. The entire island was thick with trees, and there were any number of places for someone to hide and ambush an unsuspecting visitor walking down the path.

"If this man is legit, he'll recommend some place more public, if for no other reason than his own protection. For all he knows, this is a scam on your part and you're planning to rob him. Of course," he added, "you're not really meeting him. I'll get a female agent to stand in for you."

There was a part of her that would have loved to let someone else take her place, but Mackenzie knew that wasn't possible. "Whoever did this was a friend of my father's. He knows I was the one who placed the ad, and I'll be the one he expects to see when he shows up at the memorial. If there's an agent there instead, he's going to smell a setup and bolt."

She was right, but Patrick didn't like it. "I can't let you take that kind of chance."

"What chance? He's a history buff," she reminded him. "He's not going to kill anyone over a handwritten note from FDR."

She had a point, but he wasn't ready to completely concede—not yet, anyway. "We'll see," he said, "but first we have to see if Mr. Lyons—or whatever the hell his name is—takes the bait."

"There's only way to find out," Mackenzie said, and sent the e-mail into cyberspace.

The last thing either of them expected was an almost immediate response. *Tomorrow at ten is fine. See you there.*

Surprised, Patrick whistled softly. "That was quick.

Looks like someone is really anxious to get their hands on some stolen merchandise."

"He didn't even blink at meeting at the island," she said, amazed. "You think this is the thief, don't you?"

"Oh, yeah," he said, pleased. "He's got to be really desperate to take such a risk."

"So now what?"

"I've got to line up some help and make arrangements," he said, reaching for his cell phone. "We're not walking into this without backup."

Because the National Archives' Office of Inspector General was only a three person operation, Patrick called his brother, Logan, who was an FBI agent, for help. An hour later, the arrangements were made. Patrick, Logan and three other agents would stake out the island in the morning, before Mackenzie arrived for her meeting with the man who they could only wrongly refer to as Hunter Lyons. Everyone knew what they had to do. Now all they could do was wait.

"Have you eaten?" Patrick asked her as she shut down the computer. "We could go down to Chester's, if you like…"

Chester's was three blocks away and famous for its burgers, but Mackenzie's stomach rolled just at the thought of food. "I'm sorry. I'm really not hungry. It's been an emotional day."

"I know what you mean," he said huskily. Reaching for her, he pulled her into his arms and wrapped her close. "I'll tell you about mine if you tell me about yours."

Burying her face against his neck, she smiled faintly. "You first. I don't know if I can talk about it yet."

"That bad, huh?"

"Not bad," she said huskily. "Just emotional. You know...one of those epiphanies that sort of turns your world upside down."

"Actually, I do know," he said. "I had a meeting with Carla today."

Pulling back, she gave him an arch look. "You saw your ex today?"

Watching the emotions flicker in her eyes, Patrick made no attempt to hold back a grin. "I don't know what's going on in your head, but if you think there's something going on between me and Carla, that's not happening. Though we did make peace," he added, "of a sort. She wants me back in Tommy's life."

Stunned, she gasped, "Are you serious?"

"She's willing to put it in writing and file it with the courts. My lawyer's already drawing up the paperwork."

"Oh, my God, Patrick, that's wonderful!"

Shoving his hands in the pockets of his jacket, he stared off into the distance, to that moment he'd walked away from Carla in absolute fury and she'd called after him, changing everything with a promise he'd never expected from her. "I'm still not sure I trust her, but I've never seen her like this before. She's in hell right now."

"She destroyed her family," Mackenzie said quietly. "Even if she wasn't happy with your marriage, she didn't have to end things the way she did. She must be carrying around an incredible amount of guilt."

"She is. That, alone, was a surprise. I didn't think she was capable of thinking about anyone but herself."

"She's a mother," Mackenzie said simply. "She did the right thing for her son. When do you get to see him?"

"We haven't even talked about that," he said with a wry smile. "I was afraid to push it until all the paperwork was done. I didn't want her to change her mind."

"She obviously loves her son very much. She's not going to change her mind." Happy for him, she kissed him softly on the mouth. "Congratulations. You must be walking on air."

"I am." Grinning, he snatched her off her feet, surprising a laugh from her. "I worked this afternoon, but I can't remember a damn thing I did." Kissing her fiercely, he carried her into the small living room and sank down to the couch with her in his arms. "Mmm. You taste pretty damn good, Ms. Sloan."

"So do you," she said, kissing him back.

He could have kissed her for hours, but he hadn't forgotten the emotions clouding her eyes when she'd talked about her day. Cradling her close, he said gruffly, "So...tell me about your epiphany. It was obviously painful. What happened?"

She wanted, needed, to tell him, but she couldn't. Not now. Not when he was still so high about getting his son back. She didn't want to talk about the longing, the fear tearing her apart. This was his night, and she wasn't going to bring him down by wallowing in self-pity and dwelling on the past.

"It's..." She hesitated, then made a face as tears stung her eyes. "I'm sorry. I didn't mean to be such a crybaby."

"Don't be silly," he murmured, gently wiping away the tears that spilled over her lashes. "Cry if you need to. We don't have to talk about this now, you know. If it's too upsetting, you can tell me another time. Or you don't have to tell me at all. It's totally up to you."

"No, I want to tell you." She sniffed. "Just not now when I feel like I'm falling apart. I'm sorry. My emotions are all over the map and—"

"Shh," he said softly, pressing a whisper of a kiss to her mouth. "You don't have to say anything else. Just close your eyes and relax and let me take care of everything."

"But I should—"

His mouth closed over hers, whisper-soft, seducing her with a tenderness that had pleasure rippling through her. She moaned softly and sank into his arms. "You don't play fair."

"You ain't seen nothing yet," he growled, and kissed her again. And before she could guess his intentions, he twisted and fell backwards on the couch, pulling her down with him. In little more than seconds, she found herself sprawled on top of him, her legs tangling with his.

"Patrick!" She laughed. "What—"

Tangling his fingers in her hair, he pulled her down to him and kissed her playfully, nuzzling her neck and ear until she giggled and squirmed. She was still giggling when he suddenly rolled and switched their positions. "Wait!" she cried, laughing. "We're going to roll off the couch."

"Not a chance." He chuckled and captured her hands to pull them over her head and anchor them to the couch pillows above her head. "See. I've got you."

Grinning, she teased, "What? No handcuffs?"

"We'll get to that later," he promised, and with sudden, intense care, trailed a single finger down the center of her body.

Just that easily, he stole her smile and had her throbbing in less than sixty seconds flat.

Stunned, her heart hammering, Mackenzie tried to remember why she shouldn't do this, why she couldn't let herself want him, need him so much. But it was too late for that. Somehow, he'd stolen her heart, and later, she knew that was going to keep her awake nights. But she couldn't worry about that now, not when her heart was in his hands and all she wanted to do was give in to the passion burning in her like a fast-racing fire fanned by a desert wind.

Her heart pounding, she reached for him eagerly, desperate to claim him. Pulling him back down to her, she kissed him hungrily, her fingers blindly tugging at his jacket, his shirt, the snap of his jeans. She wanted to touch, to taste, to destroy what was left of his control.

His jacket came off and went flying, then his flannel shirt and jeans. Growling low in his throat, he reached for the hem of her sweater and swiftly pulled it over her head. It hadn't even hit the floor when his hands moved to the snap of her bra. She was still gasping when he tossed it aside and unzipped her jeans.

Then his strong, knowing hands were on her, racing across her naked breasts, her hips, stroking, rubbing, seducing. She moaned, her breathing ragged as she reached for him, pulling him down to her, into her. Then they were moving together, hips pumping, their bodies hot and slick and in perfect rhythm as need clawed at them with sharp talons, tearing at control, sanity. When the sweet, hot fire flashed between them, their mingled cries shattered the silence of the night as they collapsed in each other's arms, shuddering.

He didn't ever want to move again.

At some point, they'd turned off the lights, and as they snuggled like two spoons under the throw that had been carelessly tossed over the back of the couch, Patrick could have lain there with her for days on end and never felt the need to be anywhere else. And he didn't have a clue how that had happened. What had she done to him? He'd sworn he'd never trust a woman again, but when he was with her, none of that seemed to matter. All he could think about was holding her, kissing her, making love with her.

It's just sex.

Right on schedule, the irritating voice in his head spoke up and tried to drag him back to reality, but he wasn't buying it. Not this time. He'd had sex plenty of times, and what they'd shared was a hell of a long way from just sex. It was…

Immediately shying away from putting a name to it, he told himself he wasn't going there. Not now. Maybe never. A man didn't need to put labels on every damn thing. Whatever was going on between him and Mackenzie was pretty damn fine. For now, that was enough.

But as he draped his arm over her waist and buried his face in her hair, a fist of emotions tightened around his heart, and he knew he wasn't fooling anyone, least of all himself. Did she know what she did to him? That he couldn't stop touching her? That he was going to dream of her like this…and wake in the middle of the night reaching for her? Would she do the same? Would she call his name in the night?

In the darkness, she slowly, absently, stroked his arm. "Patrick?"

His hand covered hers; their fingers linked and gently held. "Hmm?"

"Earlier, when I told you I couldn't talk about my day…"

"You had a rough day," he said quietly. "You don't have to talk about it, sweetheart. It's okay."

For a moment, he thought she was going to let it go. Content to hold his hand in the darkness, she let the silence of the night stretch between them. And as she once again relaxed in his arms, he thought she'd fallen asleep. Then she said quietly, "My mother died in childbirth when I was twelve."

Whatever he was expecting her to say, it wasn't that. Instinctively, his arm tightened around her waist, pulling her closer back against him. "That must have been incredibly difficult for you and your father."

She told him about the ice storm that hit the same day her mother went into labor. "We lived in Richmond, then, out in the country, and Dad was out of town at a convention," she said huskily. "He was coming home that night, and I realize now that once Mom knew she was in labor, she thought he would be home long before the baby came."

"But he wasn't?"

Wrapped in his arms, she shook her head. "He couldn't make it in because of the storm."

Cradling her close, he rested his cheek against hers. "So what did your mother do? Drive herself to the hospital?"

"No, I did."

"You were twelve!"

Her watery laugh balanced on a sob. "You do what you have to do. She couldn't drive, so I did…very, very slowly."

"But you didn't make it?"

"No."

Shocked, he said, "Are you telling you were all alone with your mom on the side of the road somewhere when she died?"

"No. I didn't get very far before Mom realized just how bad the roads were, so I turned around and we went back to the house."

"Oh, sweetheart, you must have been terrified!"

"I tried to help her," she choked out, "but I was *twelve!* And in the long run, it didn't matter what I did. The baby was breech. I called 911, and fifteen minutes later, air rescue arrived, but it was too late. A blood clot went to Mom's heart and she died."

He swore softly. "The baby died, too, didn't it?" She couldn't speak, couldn't do anything but nod, and his heart broke for her. "I can't even imagine what that must have been like for you," he said gruffly. "I'm so sorry."

Holding tightly to him, she struggled to force back tears. "It was the most devastating thing that ever happened to me or my father. Dad never really got over it, even after he sold the house and moved us to D.C."

"What about you? You lost your mother."

"I swore I was never having children," she said simply, "and I thought I was okay with that. Then I went with Stacy to the doctor today for a sonogram."

"She's okay, isn't she?"

"She's healthy as a horse," she replied. "And the baby is, too."

Patrick twined his fingers with hers. "Thank God for that. So what's the problem? Why are you upset? You must be relieved that's everything's okay?"

"Oh, I am," she said quickly. "I just wasn't expecting…" She hesitated, her voice suddenly thick with emotion when she said, "Stacy's like a sister to me— the only family I have left. Ever since I found out she was pregnant, all I've been able to think about is I'm going to lose her like I lost my mother…because of the pregnancy. Then…I s-saw the s-sonogram—"

"And saw a baby," he guessed when she couldn't seem to find the right words.

In the darkness, tears spilled over her lashes. "She just became so real," she said thickly. "She's a baby. Just a sweet, innocent baby. And if things were different—"

I could have one, too.

She didn't say the words, but Patrick heard them nevertheless. His heart aching for her, he kissed her damp cheek and tasted her tears. "Watching your mother die had to be the most horrible thing anyone can witness, especially considering the way she died. No one can blame you for deciding after that to never have children. I'd have been surprised if you hadn't."

"I missed my mother so much. I didn't want to take

a chance that a child of mine might go through the same thing I did. I couldn't risk that."

"It's a perfectly logical conclusion," he agreed. "But you were twelve. You're an adult now. And you have to know that what happened to your mother was incredibly rare then and now."

"But it could happen again."

"Possibly," he said with a shrug. "But what are the odds of a woman dying in childbirth, then her daughter suffering the same fate decades later? Probably slim to none. You have to decide if you want to take those odds."

It was as simple as that. And when she didn't, couldn't, respond, he realized she didn't have a clue what she was going to do.

Chapter 12

Her heart in her throat, Mackenzie followed the signs to the Theodore Roosevelt Memorial and wasn't surprised to discover that the parking lot was deserted. It was barely nine o'clock in the morning and hardly the kind of day that even the most ardent nature-lover would venture out into. It was thirty-six degrees, and a cold drizzle had been falling since dawn.

Huddling in her coat, she shivered. With a canoe tied to the top of his SUV, Patrick had left forty-five minutes before her, driving to a parking area upstream from Theodore Roosevelt Island, where he had met with a handful of FBI agents and canoed downstream to the island. By now, she knew, they were carefully hidden in the trees, ready to arrest Hunter Lyons—or whatever his name was—if he was foolish enough to show up.

Staring at the thick stand of trees that began at the edge of the parking lot, she could almost feel the touch of eyes on her. Her blood running cold, she told herself she had nothing to fear. Patrick and his men were within shouting distance, and at Patrick's insistence, she was wearing a bulletproof vest and wired for sound. If she so much as drew in a sharp breath, Mr. Lyons was going to find himself surrounded and looking down the barrels of more than a few guns. Knowing that, however, did nothing to still the trembling of her fingers as she unbuckled her seat belt and reached for the door handle.

Secluded and quiet in spite of the fact that it was right across the river from Washington, D.C., the island appeared to be nearly untouched by time. There was, however, no time to appreciate the serenity of the place. The pathway that led to the memorial beckoned, and with her heart in her throat, Mackenzie opened her umbrella and headed into the trees.

Under any other circumstances, the walk would have been incredibly peaceful, but she couldn't appreciate the quiet of the place for the fear that gripped her by the throat. A branch snapped in the trees to her right, startling her. Fighting the need to run, she froze. Was that someone in the trees up ahead, watching her? Where was Patrick? And the other agents? Could they see her? Were they even really there? What if something had happened to hold them up? What if—

"You're all right," Patrick said quietly through the earpiece in her ear. "Harry just stepped on a branch."

Tears spilling into her eyes, she almost wilted right where she stood. Wishing she could step into his arms, knowing she couldn't, she started down the path again, her eyes searching the trees that blended one into another. "Where are you?" she asked shakily in a whisper that was so soft it didn't even carry to her own ears.

"Forty-five degrees to your left," he said just as softly. "Near the top of the ridge."

Trying to disguise where she was looking in case Lyons was also somewhere in the trees, watching her as she made her way to the memorial, she moved just her eyes and searched the top of the ridge to her left. For a long moment, she saw nothing but trees. Then, just when she was about to give up hope of spotting him, something moved twenty feet below the crest of the ridge. It was barely a whisper of movement that she would have missed if she'd blinked, a quick smile from Patrick as he peeked out at her from his hiding place. Just as quickly as he appeared, he was gone, blending back into the natural camouflage that surrounded him without appearing to move at all.

Relieved, she started to smile, only to remember that there was a very good possibility that Lyons was watching. If he saw even a hint of relief on her face, he'd know not only that she wasn't there alone, but that he'd been set up.

Her heart pounding, she continued toward the memorial and could have sworn she heard movement behind her. She wanted to believe it was Patrick or one of the other agents, but they'd been so careful to blend in with their surroundings, she knew they wouldn't have made that kind of mistake.

Nerves jumping in her stomach, she fought the

need to look behind her even as she picked up her pace. Unfortunately, a sting operation couldn't be rushed, and once she reached the memorial, there was nothing she could do but wait. Then wait some more. Ten o'clock came and went, and there was still no sign of Lyons or anyone else. The weather worsened, and the drizzle that had cast a gray pall over everything became an icy downpour.

Her umbrella doing nothing to protect her from the damp, miserable cold that seemed to eat into her bones, Mackenzie shivered. Just when she didn't think she could take it anymore, Patrick growled in her ear, "This is a wash. Let's get the hell out of here."

"Are you sure?" she argued. "Maybe we should give him a few more minutes. With the roads so slick, there are bound to be a lot of accidents. He could have got caught in traffic or something."

"If he came at all," Patrick said. "He might have got cold feet. Or he was here long before any of us and saw us coming down the river. Either way, there's no point in staying. He's not here."

The decision made, Patrick and the rest of the agents stepped out of the trees and made their way to where Mackenzie waited at the memorial. For the first time, she understood how they blended into the trees so easily. They were all decked out in camo.

Even though they were dressed appropriately for the weather, there was no question that they were chilled to the bone. Water dripped from their caps and noses and eye-lashes, but not a one of them issued a word of complaint.

"You must all be frozen solid," she said huskily.

"I'm sorry you had to come out in this kind of weather for nothing."

"Don't worry about it," Patrick's brother Logan told her. "If nothing else, we learned that this Lyons character is a liar and either knows he's under investigation or is very skittish. Either way, it's only a matter of time before he makes a mistake that leads us right to him. We just have to be patient.

"And it was worth it to see Patrick get out in the field and do some real work for a change," he added with a grin.

"Hey! I work!"

"Oh, yeah," he teased. "I've seen how you work up a sweat at those memorabilia shows you go to. You're working real hard, big brother."

"You're just jealous," Patrick retorted, chuckling.

"Jealous?!" he snorted. "Yeah, right. And why the hell would I be jealous?"

"Because the idiots you arrest are dumb as a rock and no challenge at all. At least the perps I deal with are educated and have a brain. I have to actually think to catch them."

"So what happened this morning, Einstein?" Logan tossed back, grinning broadly.

"Okay." He laughed. "So sometimes I get out-smarted. Are we having fun yet?"

"Oh, yeah, I'm having a lot of fun this morning," Logan said dryly. "If we don't all come down with pneumonia, we can do this again the next time your perp decides to exercise his brain. Thanks a lot."

"I do what I can." Patrick chuckled.

His green eyes twinkling, Logan turned to Mackenzie. "The next time he decides to think, call us, Mac. We'll do what we can to help. He's the oldest, you know. Mom didn't know what she was doing when she had him. He was the test model. The rest of us turned out much better."

Mackenzie laughed. "Somehow, I have a feeling he'd disagree with you."

"You're damn straight," Patrick retorted. "The first-born gets all the brain cells. You'd know that if you weren't the second born."

Logan teasingly gave him a rude hand gesture. "Try to stay out of trouble, Einstein. Call me if you need me. Mac, we'll have to do this again."

"Hey, take the canoe back for me, okay?" Patrick called after him as he and the other agents stepped into the trees and headed for the boats that had been used to bring them to the island. "I'll be by later to pick it up."

"Don't worry about it," his brother called back to him. "I'll drop it by your place."

Within seconds, they'd disappeared from view, leaving Patrick and Mackenzie in the peaceful silence of the memorial. "Well, that's that," Mackenzie said ruefully. "It's back to square one."

"Don't let this get you down," Patrick told her, pulling her close for a hug. "We knew there was a possibility that he wouldn't show. That doesn't mean we're not going to catch him."

"I know," she sighed. "But when? He always seems to be one step ahead of us."

"Maybe for now," he agreed, "but his luck's eventually going to run out. We just have to regroup and try again."

"He's not going to answer another ad."

"No, but we'll just come after him from a different direction. And remember, he wants the stolen items back. If he wants those documents back badly enough, we won't have to find him. He'll find us."

"I can't believe this man may be one of my father's friends!" she said, frustrated. "Somebody he trusted, for God's sake! He probably cried at his funeral and told me how sorry he was. You would think tracking him down would be easy."

"And maybe that's the problem," Patrick argued as they headed for her car. "He's obviously on to us—he knows we're aware of the fact that he's a friend of your father's. So he's going to do everything he can to make sure we don't figure out who he is. He might not be nearly as cautious, though, with other people."

She frowned. "Other people? Like who?"

"Your dad wasn't his only customer," he pointed out. "He didn't steal all the documents he did just to lock them up in a safe somewhere. He sold them, and probably for a hell of a lot less than they were worth. Which means," he added, "that buyers looking to make a good profit put them right back on the market. All we have to do is find them."

"So what are you saying? We check eBay? Memorabilia shows? And hope we get lucky?"

He didn't have to tell her the odds on them being at the right show at the right time to confiscate the stolen documents were slim to none. And even if they were able to recover the items, that didn't mean they would necessarily be able to trace them back to the thief. So far, the man had been damned elusive and far more clever than the average criminal. Patrick didn't mind admitting that worried him. What else had the bastard stolen that belonged to the American people? And how much of it had already ended up in the hands of private collectors and would never be seen again?

"Are we fighting a losing battle here?"

Looking up from his thoughts, he found Mackenzie studying him with searching blue eyes that saw far too much. "Tell me the truth, Patrick. There's a possibility we may never catch this guy, isn't there?"

He hesitated. "I don't like the word *never,*" he said finally, "but yes, there's always that possibility. Sometimes we catch the perp but never retrieve the stolen documents. Sometimes we track down the document but never catch the perp. And other times, we hit nothing but a brick wall. All we can do is turn over every stone and keep looking."

They reached her PT Cruiser then, and she lifted a brow at him as he opened her car door for her. "So where do we start?"

"My office," he said promptly. "Can you go back to the office with me? We need sit down together and go over your father's file. You know more about his business that I do. Maybe you'll catch something I didn't."

"Of course," she said, surprised. "I'll be happy to do whatever I can."

As he joined her in the car, however, and she pulled out of the parking lot, she added, "Not that I'll be able to help you much. The jackass who did this is a friend of my father's, for God's sake. I should know who he is. What am I missing?"

"It's not just you," he said. "I talked to every one

of those men, and I would have sworn none of them had a dishonest bone in their body. Either one of them's a damn good liar, or I missed something major. Do you know if any of them are having any financial problems? Are any of them sick, going through a divorce—"

When he abruptly broke off in midsentence, Mackenzie took her eyes off the road for a split second and glanced over to find him staring out the side window, scowling. "What is it?" she asked, surprised. "What's wrong?"

"That jogger we just passed," he said, glancing back over his shoulder at the runner who'd just jogged past them at an easy pace on the bike path that ran parallel to the road. "She looks like someone I work with at the Archives."

"You didn't know she was a runner?"

"No, it's just… Turn around," he said abruptly. "If that's the woman I think it is, she lives in Baltimore and commutes every day. What's she doing jogging in D.C. on a Saturday?"

"Maybe she had business in town and decided to get a run in while she was here. Why?" she asked with a frown even as she exited the parkway and circled back the way they had come. "What difference does it make?"

"We're only a couple of miles from the TR Memorial," he pointed out. "And if that's who I think it is, she works in the department that handles new acquisitions."

When Mackenzie still didn't make the connection, he explained, "She records new acquisitions. Nothing I recovered at your shop or you sold on eBay had been recorded. That's why they were so easy to sell. There were no file notes, nothing to indicate that they were stolen and belonged to the Archives."

"So what are you saying? She stole documents before they were recorded so no one knew they were there to begin with? That makes sense, but how does this have anything to do with my father? She wasn't a friend of my father's—"

"How do you know that?"

"Because—" Hesitating, she frowned. "If by *friend,* you mean they were romantically involved…"

"Someone had a key to the shop and the code to the security system," he pointed out. "Like you, I thought he gave it to a friend in case something happened to him and just assumed it was one of his poker buddies. But a woman makes more sense."

Not sure how she felt about the idea, Mackenzie couldn't wrap her mind around the idea of her father dating someone. He'd dated after he'd gotten over her mother's death, but he'd never been serious about anyone. As far as Mackenzie knew, up until the day he died, he'd never loved anyone but her mother.

"There was no woman at his funeral," she argued. "And none of his poker buddies mentioned her when you questioned them," she reminded him. "He would have told me if he was involved with someone."

"Even if she was a lot younger than he was?"

Shooting him a narrow-eyed look, she said, "How much younger?"

"Twenty years."

"What?"

"I know," he said quickly when outrage sparked in

her eyes. "You think your father would never do such a thing. But your mother died a long time ago. Your dad had to be lonely—"

"No."

"People do crazy things sometimes."

"No."

"She's young and pretty. Any man would have been flattered."

"Never in a million years," she said flatly. "He wouldn't be that foolish."

She couldn't have been more adamant, but Patrick wasn't convinced she was right. She'd lived halfway across the country, and hadn't seen her father that often over the course of the past few years. She couldn't have possibly known what was going on in his personal life. And even if she thought she did, daughters didn't always see their fathers for who they really were.

"Let's say for the sake of argument that you're right and there was no romantic relationship. They still could have been friends. When your father became ill, he probably wanted someone he trusted to have a key and the alarm code in case something happened to him."

"And in return for trusting her, she sold him stolen documents?" she tossed back. "What kind of friend is that?"

"That's what we're going to find out," he said grimly as they approached the jogger and he got another look at the woman. "Because that sure as hell is Leslie Shue, and she's headed straight for T.R.'s memorial."

Trying not to stare as she passed the woman, Mackenzie tightened her hands on the wheel. "So what do we do now?"

"Head for the Archives," he said flatly. "While she's checking us out, we'll check the lady out and see if we can figure out what she's up to."

It wasn't difficult to get into Leslie Shue's office. Patrick simply called security and ordered the guard to unlock her office door and her desk. Two minutes later, he started to swear. "Son of a bitch!"

"What?" Mackenzie asked, standing next to the guard in the doorway. "What's wrong? What did you find?"

"More of Washington's papers," he replied in disgust. "They look like they're from the same batch your father had." Carefully flipping through some of the other documents, he held up a newspaper clipping. "Here's a copy of your ad in *The Patriot.*"

"Are you serious?"

He nodded grimly. "She circled it. Damn! I can't believe I missed this! I should have seen—"

"How?" she demanded. "God only knows how many documents in the Archives aren't recorded. And Dad was studying the same group of documents. Why would you be suspicious of an Archives employee when everything pointed to Dad?"

"Because none of the stolen items were recorded. That should have immediately tipped me off that it was an inside job. Your dad, though, was just so obvious. And I'm sure that was what Leslie was counting on."

Just thinking about how he'd missed what was right in front of his nose, he swore again. "She had the perfect opportunity. No one questioned her authority—she had free rein to take what she wanted without anyone suspecting what she was doing because she was the only one who knew what had come in."

"So what do you do now? Confront her?"

"Not yet," he said grimly. "I've got to move quickly to search her house and bank accounts before she realizes we're on to her and disposes of the evidence."

Horrified, Mackenzie gasped, "Do you really think she'd do that? She works for the Archives, for heaven's sake! How could she destroy the very thing she gets paid to preserve?"

He shrugged. "When push comes to shove, most people will do whatever they have to to stay out of prison. I've caught thieves who would have burned the Declaration of Independence without a blink of an eye rather than chance getting caught with it and spending the rest of their life in prison."

"Are you serious?"

"Never underestimate a desperate man…or woman," he added grimly. "Some people give up the second I show up on their doorstep. Others run and sometimes throw guns into the equation. We have to be ready for anything."

Instructing the guard to change Leslie Shue's access code to the building and to call him immediately if she showed up, he turned back to Mackenzie. "I've got a lot of work to do in the next few hours," he told her. "Are you going to be okay?"

"I'll be fine," she assured him as they headed for the exit. "Especially now that I know this woman is about to be caught. Stacy and I are going shopping for items for the nursery after we take John to the airport."

Surprised, he lifted a dark brow. "He's going on another business trip this close to Christmas? Isn't the baby due soon?"

"Not for nearly a month, but he's only going to be gone for a few nights. He'll be back on Wednesday and won't be going anywhere until six weeks after the baby is born."

His green eyes searching hers, he frowned. "How are you dealing with this? You're still worried about the baby, aren't you?"

A rueful smile curled the corners of her mouth. "Is it that obvious?"

"Only when you frown…and smile…and breathe."

"I'm not that bad!" She laughed. "Am I?"

It was that quiet *Am I?* that had him reaching for her. "Everything's going to be fine," he said huskily. "You'll see. The baby will put in an appearance when she's good and ready, then we'll all go out and celebrate. Okay? So go pick out some gorgeous furniture for your goddaughter while I find out everything I can about Leslie Shue and her illegal activities over the last few years. Then we can put all this behind us."

And do what? she wanted to ask, but there was no time. He had to get back to his case and she had to pick up Stacy and John and drive John to the airport. Glancing at her watch, she gasped. "I've got to go," she said, giving him a kiss. "I'm late."

"Be careful," he called after her. "I'll call you later."

* * *

The airport was packed, the traffic backed up and crazy. Mackenzie let John and Stacy off at the terminal, then went in search of short-term parking. By the time she located a parking space and hurried back to the terminal and the security check where John and Stacy waited, John only had seconds to say goodbye.

"Remember what the doctor said," he told Stacy as he hugged her. "One hour of shopping for the baby, then nothing but rest until the baby's born. No more shopping, no housecleaning, no running around. You get in bed, put your feet up and don't budge except to go to the bathroom. Understood?"

Tears welling in her eyes, she gave him a watery smile and saluted smartly. "Yes, sir. Whatever you say, Mr. Green."

Grinning, he pulled her into his arms for one last kiss. "I'll give you Mr. Green, Mrs. Green. Don't get sassy with me." Glancing at Mackenzie, he said, "Take care of her, Mac. I'll be back as quick as I can."

Stacy insisted on staying until he made it through security, then couldn't hold back tears as she and Mackenzie made their way to short-term parking. "Wednesday will be here before you know it," Mackenzie assured her. "We'll have the nursery completely done by then." Grinning wryly, she added, "I guess I should say *I'll* have the nursery completed. You have to rest or John will have my hide when he gets back."

"I don't sleep when he's gone." She sniffed, wiping away her tears. "I know it's silly, but I miss him already."

"That's not silly." Mackenzie chuckled, taking her

eyes off the road for a second to grin at her. "You love him and you want him with you. And you're pregnant, for heaven's sake. Your emotions are all over the m—"

The truck that ran the red light on the cross street never even slowed down. Shooting into the intersection at fifty miles per hour, it slammed into Mackenzie's PT Cruiser and nearly knocked it off its wheels.

Later, Mackenzie didn't remember screaming. Then her car crashed into a telephone pole on the far corner of the intersection and her head cracked against her side window. Pain, sharp as a knife, stabbed her in the head. Before she could do anything but gasp, darkness hit her like a freight train.

Chapter 13

"Oh, God! Oh, God! The baby... I can't lose my baby!"

Her head throbbing, Mackenzie drifted back to consciousness to the sound of Stacy's frantic cries. For a moment, her words didn't register. Then Mackenzie's heart stopped cold in her breast. "The baby! Oh, God!"

Old memories swamping her, horrifying her, she struggled to unsnap her seat belt with fingers that were far from steady. "Hang on, Stace. Help is coming. I hear an ambulance—"

Her face white as parchment and tears streaming from her eyes, Stacy held a protective hand to her swollen stomach. "Something's wrong, Mac. The baby—I'm so scared!"

Unaware of the blood trailing from a cut near her hairline, Mackenzie finally fought free of her seat belt, then reached for Stacy's. "We're not going to lose another baby!" she said fiercely. "Do you hear me? History isn't repeating itself! I won't let it."

Closing her eyes as a contraction hit her, Stacy fought for control. "You're right. We're going to be all right. I've got to believe that."

"That's right. Just breathe. Nice slow, steady breaths."

"Oh, God, I'm so scared."

Tears stung Mackenzie's eyes. "I know. Me, too."

She was, in fact, terrified. She could see her mother's face all those years ago as the pain of one contraction after another ripped through her. Mackenzie had never felt so helpless before or since...until now. "Dammit, where's that ambulance?" she choked out. "We've got to get you to the hospital."

The words were hardly out of her mouth when people seemed to suddenly come running from all directions. Mackenzie's door was pulled almost at the same time Stacy's was, then an EMT was kneeling in front of her, checking her head, asking her questions that frustrated her past bearing.

"I'm not the one who's hurt," she cried. "It's my friend. She's pregnant. The baby's coming!"

"She's in good hands," the young EMT assured her. "Right now, let's get you checked out. Are you hurt anywhere else besides your head?"

"My head? What are you talking about? I—" She lifted a hand to her temple, only to wince at the sudden, sharp pain in her head. When she pulled back her fingers, they were dripping in blood.

Horrified, she stared at the bright crimson of her

own blood and suddenly couldn't seem to focus. She heard a roaring in her ears, and without a sound, she passed out cold.

When she came to a few short moments later, she was strapped onto a stretcher and being loaded into a waiting ambulance. Confused, she looked around frantically for Stacy. "Wait!" she cried. "Stacy—"

"She's already on her way to the hospital," the EMT told her.

"Is she okay? The baby?"

"We don't know yet," he told her as he climbed in beside her in the ambulance. "She appears to be in labor."

"Oh, God!" Tears welled in her eyes and spilled over her lashes. "This is my fault. I should have been more careful."

"How is it your fault when some idiot runs a light?" he asked practically. "You're both lucky to be alive."

"But it's too soon for the baby! If something happens to her—"

"We've got one of the best obstetrics and neonatal units in the country," he assured her. "Trust me, mother and baby will both be fine. Right now, the only thing you have to worry about is taking care of you. If you don't calm down, I'm going to have to give you a sedative—"

"No!" Agitated, she grabbed his hand. "You don't understand. Stacy's husband flew out an hour ago for New York. This is her first baby, and she doesn't have anyone else but me. I have to be okay. She can't go through this alone."

"We'll talk about it when we get to the hospital and see how you are," he promised. "But you're not going to be any good to her or yourself if you're bleeding all over the place and passing out on her. Okay?"

He was right. She knew he was right, but she was so scared. Dragging in a deep breath, she nodded. "Okay. I'm sorry."

"There's no need to apologize," he told her. "You're worried about your friend. What about you? Is there someone I can call for you?"

"Patrick." His name popped out before she even stopped to think that he was probably, at that very moment, up to his eyebrows in the investigation and, hopefully, the arrest of Leslie Shue. "No," she said quickly. "He's working. He can't come right now."

"Maybe you should let him tell you that," he advised quietly. "I can give him a call for you."

He had no idea how he tempted her. But as much as she wanted to give him Patrick's number, arresting the woman who had set up her father was more important. "No," she said with a wistful smile. "I'll see him later."

"Have it your way," he said with a shrug. "If you change your mind, just let me know."

Leslie Shue lived in a modest house in Silver Spring, Maryland. Meeting with his brother Logan and the other agents who'd staked out Theodore Roosevelt Island earlier that morning, Patrick said flatly, "She's home. She has to know that she's looking at significant jail time if she's caught, so be prepared for anything."

"Give us ten minutes to surround the house," Logan said. "You've got the search warrant?"

Patrick nodded. "I found a hell of a lot of evidence in her office, including a letter sent from Jefferson to Washington on the eve of Washington's inauguration. It would be worth a small fortune on the open market, and she'd hidden it in the lining of a jacket hanging in her coat closet. Apparently, that was how she got the documents out of the building."

"How long has she worked at the Archives?"

"Six years."

Logan whistled softly. "That's a hell of a lot of time to help yourself to national treasures."

Patrick agreed. "If we recover half of it, we'll be lucky." His face carved in harsh lines, he said, "C'mon, let's do it."

Together, they approached the front door, but it was Patrick who hammered on the door. For a few long seconds, he was afraid Leslie would run—he could clearly hear movement on the other side of the door—but then the sound of the dead bolt sliding free had him bracing for action. If she was stupid enough to have a gun—

He needn't have worried. Slowly pulling the door open, Leslie stood before him as white as a sheet, her hands empty, her eyes dark with despair. "How did you know it was me?"

"I saw you jogging this morning, and couldn't come up with a reason why you would be anywhere near Roosevelt Island on a Saturday. Then I remembered what your job was and put two and two together." Studying her curiously, he said, "What was your relationship with Michael Sloan? Were you dating? Or were you just using him to fence what you stole?"

Lifting her chin a fraction, she said, "Michael and I were friends—"

"Did he know the documents you sold him were stolen?"

"Of course not! He would have never—" Breaking off abruptly, she obviously decided she'd said enough. "I have nothing more to say to you. I want a lawyer."

Not surprised, Patrick shrugged. "If that's the way you want to play it, I can't stop you, but it's in your best interest to cooperate." When she just looked at him, he read her her rights. "You have the right to remain silent…"

Logan handcuffed her, and within minutes, Patrick and the rest of the agents from the FBI were going through Leslie's house with a fine-tooth comb, turning the place upside down in search of stolen documents, maps and rare books. Not surprisingly, a search of Leslie's clothes turned up a dozen maps from the American Revolution and Civil War hidden in the lining of her jackets and secret pockets in her slacks and skirts. Then one of the agents discovered a loose floorboard in the bottom of her bedroom closet. When it was pried up, they found a stash of books worth a small fortune that were covered in mold.

Furious, Patrick was still swearing five minutes later when Devin called. Snapping open his phone, he said, "I can't talk right now. We made an arrest in the Sloan case and we're right in the middle of recovering some of the archival documents—"

"Mackenzie's been in an accident, Patrick."

His gaze directed on one of the molded books that looked like it would be a total loss, it was several long seconds before his brother's words registered. "What? Is she all right? What happened? Where is she?"

"St. Joseph's," Devin said promptly. "A drunk driver ran a light and plowed into her. I just heard about it on my radio. I thought you'd want to know."

"I'm on my way," he said hoarsely. Snapping his phone shut, he turned, worry already eating a hole in his gut, and almost ran into Logan. His brother took one look at his face, and said sharply, "What is it? What's wrong?"

"Mackenzie," he said hoarsely. "She's been in an accident. Devin just called to tell me. She was hit by a drunk driver."

"Go," his brother said gruffly. "I'll take care of everything here."

He didn't have to tell him twice. Already out the door, Patrick ran for his car.

The emergency room was packed due to a ten-car pileup on the Beltway, so it was several long moments before Patrick was able to find anyone who could tell him anything about Mackenzie. "She was in here about thirty minutes ago," a nurse told him, "but her friend was upstairs having her baby. The second I got her patched up, she ran upstairs."

"Stacy's in labor?" Swearing, Patrick thanked her for her help. "Where's labor and delivery?"

"Seventh floor." The words were hardly out of her mouth when he turned to run for the elevator. "Turn left out of the elevator," she called after him. "You can't miss it."

If the elevator doors hadn't opened at that moment,

Patrick would have taken the stairs. Even then, he found himself impatiently watching the floors tick by one by one. Silently cursing the slow-moving elevator, he sighed in relief as it finally reached the seventh floor.

"Stacy Green," he told the woman at the information desk blocking the path to the delivery rooms. "Is she still in labor? I'm looking for her friend, Mackenzie Sloan. Have you seen her? Five foot seven, curly brown hair, pretty. You can't miss her. She was in a car accident and probably has a bandage on her head."

Not bothering to check her records, the receptionist said, "Mrs. Green has been moved to her room—642— and is resting."

Patrick felt his heart turn over in his chest. "And the baby?"

"Preemie ICU," she retorted. "Down one floor. Follow the signs—they'll take you right to it."

"And Mackenzie Sloan, Stacy's friend? Have you seen her?"

"I believe she went to NICU, but she may have gone home. She looked pretty worn out."

Patrick didn't believe for a moment that Mackenzie had walked out on Stacy and the baby and gone home. "I'll check the ICU first," he said. "Thanks."

Later, he didn't even remember taking the stairs at a dead run. He reached the sixth floor and almost immediately found the nursery…and Mackenzie.

She stood with her back to him, hugging herself as she stared through the nursery window at the tiny babies in their incubators. Hurrying toward her, Patrick felt his heart constrict as he watched her wipe tears from her eyes.

He loved her.

The truth hit him then like a bolt of lightning on a clear day, knocking him out of his shoes. He loved her, and he didn't even know how it happened. After Carla had lied to him the way she had about Tommy, he'd sworn he would never trust a woman again. Then he'd walked into Mackenzie's shop and even when he had been convinced the woman was dealing in stolen Archival documents, he still hadn't been able to get her out of his head.

How had she stolen his heart without him even being aware of it?

She wiped a tear from her eye again, and then he saw the bandage on her temple. His gut clenched. How close had he come to losing her? "Mackenzie?"

She turned, her eyes still swimming with tears, at the sound of his voice. "Patrick! How did you know I was here?"

"I got a call from Devin—he heard about a wreck on his police radio," he said as he quickly closed the distance between them and reached for her. "Are you okay? The baby—"

"Oh, Patrick, she's beautiful!" Hugging him fiercely, she took his hand and pulled him closer to the nursery window. "See? She's right in the middle of the second row. Isn't she gorgeous? She looks just like Stacy."

He studied the baby with the tiny red Santa hat on her head and grinned. "If you say so. She's a cute little thing. Is she going to be okay?"

"She's going to be fine," she assured him. "The doctor said her lungs are still a little underdeveloped since she's nearly a month premature, but he's not expecting any problems."

"And what about you?" he asked huskily, gently lifting his hand to the bandage at her temple. "What happened? Are you sure you're all right?"

"I hit it on the window...I think." Telling him, her eyes clouded at the memory. "I was so scared," she admitted huskily. "I was so sure Stacy was losing the baby, and all I could think of was that history was repeating itself."

"But it didn't," he said gruffly, pulling her back into his arms. "Look at her, sweetheart. She's beautiful and healthy and so is Stacy. The nightmare's over. Everyone's safe. You don't have to worry anymore."

Hugging him fiercely, she smiled at the sight of the baby stretching in her incubator. "I know," she murmured. "The second I saw her, I felt this huge load lift from my shoulders. All I wanted to do was hold her."

Pulling back slightly, he studied her searchingly. "What's this? I didn't think you wanted anything to do with babies."

"I don't. Or at least, I didn't think I did," she admitted. "But..." Struggling for words to describe the unexpected emotions tugging at her, she said huskily, "I can't describe it, but earlier, when I was standing here by myself, watching her, I could feel my mother beside me, telling me everything was going to be all right. And I feel like it is. Whatever I decide to do, I know everything's going to be fine."

"Good," he said, pleased. "It's been a wild day—"

His phone rang then, and when he saw the call was

from his brother, he said, "I've got to take this. Hey, Logan, what'd you find?"

"You wouldn't believe what this woman had hidden in her house! We're taking the place right down to the studs, and so far, we've found over two hundred maps and rare documents, and we haven't even gone through half the house. I don't know how the hell she thought she could get away with this, but she must have been planning for retirement. Some of this stuff has to be worth a fortune!"

Patrick swore. "And that probably doesn't touch what she's already sold to private buyers that'll never be recovered."

"I wouldn't be too sure of that," Logan said. "Once we starting finding evidence hidden under her floorboards and in the walls of her house, her lawyer advised her to start cooperating. She's been spilling her guts for the last half hour."

"Are you serious? Did she say anything about her relationship with Michael Sloan?"

"Oh, yeah. Mackenzie's not going to like it, but apparently, they were involved. She met him when he was doing research at the Archives, and made a play for him. She started selling him stolen documents, claiming they were from her family's private collection, and made him promise he'd never sell them."

"So she got her money and the documents were supposed to disappear forever," Patrick concluded. "The only thing she didn't plan on was Michael Sloan dying when he did and Mackenzie selling the stolen goods on eBay."

"That was the beginning of the end and she knew it," his brother said. "The receipts she'd given Sloan for the stolen documents were damning and somewhere in his office. She knew she had to get them back and the only way she could do that was by breaking in with the security code and key Sloan had given her. She panicked, though, when she heard a siren and was afraid someone saw her inside the shop when it was closed and called the police."

"So that's why she ran out without shutting the door completely," Patrick said. "Thank God for that. If she'd closed the door, we wouldn't have had a clue anyone else had a key."

"Trust me, she's regretting it," Logan said dryly. "I've got a feeling we've only skimmed the surface of what she's stolen. I'll keep you posted on what we find."

Relieved, Patrick hung up and turned to Mackenzie, who hadn't missed a single word of his side of the conversation. "You arrested Leslie Shue!" she gasped. "Already? What happened? With the wreck and the baby and everything, I completely forgot about the investigation."

He grinned. "Based on the things we found hidden in her office, I didn't have any trouble getting a search warrant. Logan and I were at her house when Devin called and told me about your accident."

"What happened? Did Logan find something?"

"Oh, yeah," he said.

When he gave her a quick rundown of what Leslie Shue had been hiding in her house, she gasped, horrified. "Are you serious? She hid books under the floor?!

How could she have done something so stupid? She works for the Archives, for God's sake! She had to know how much that would damage them."

"Obviously, she didn't give a damn," Patrick retorted. "She just wanted to make sure she didn't get caught."

"And what did Logan say about her relationship with my father?" she asked with a frown. "Was she dating him?"

He hesitated, but there was no way around it—he had to tell her the truth. "She set your dad up, Mac. She made a play for him, got him to trust her, then sold him stolen documents she claimed were part of her family's private collection. Part of the deal was that he'd never sell the documents he'd bought from her."

Mackenzie's blue eyes flashed with outrage. "How dare she! She demands he give his word he won't sell them, and all the time she's selling him *stolen* merchandise? She's nothing but a common thief! A witch! A two-bit—"

"Yellow-bellied—" Patrick supplied, grinning.

"—road lizard," Mackenzie finished for him. "I hope you throw the book at her!"

Amused, Patrick laughed. "I'll do my best. Did I ever tell you that I love it when you get all feisty?"

Mackenzie felt her heart stop at the use of the *L* word. He didn't mean it, she told herself. Not literally. He just used it the same way people talked about chocolate or champagne. He didn't really mean he loved *her.* Did he?

Suddenly realizing that she wanted that more than she'd ever wanted anything in her life, she found herself blinking back foolish tears. When had she fallen in love with him? How? She'd been so sure that she never wanted to take that chance again, but that was before. Before Patrick swept into her world and turned her life upside down...before she stood by Stacy's side during her sonogram and found herself dealing with a longing she had been denying for years...before Patrick stole her heart and made her want...everything.

Not quite sure how to proceed, she studied him with blue eyes that were far more vulnerable than she realized. "Patrick..."

That was all she could say, just his name, and even she could hear the need in her voice. Reaching for her, he pulled her back into his arms. "I must have broken so many speed records on my way over here," he said huskily. "I kept seeing you cut and bleeding and lying half-dead in the road—"

"Oh, Patrick, no! I should have let the EMT call you, but I knew you were busy with the case and I didn't want to worry you. And I never stopped to think that Devin might hear about the accident and call you."

"You can always call me," he said roughly. "I don't care what I'm doing. Okay? I love you."

He kissed her fiercely, sweetly, with a tenderness that brought tears to her eyes. "When?" she whispered against his mouth as she kissed him back. "When did you fall in love with me?"

"The first time I walked into your shop and that damn John Philip Sousa march played." He chuckled. "You looked at me, cymbals crashed, and I was a goner."

"You're making that up!" She laughed. Then she

saw the look in his eyes and her heart turned over. "You're serious?"

"I know this may seem fast, but I couldn't stop thinking about you," he admitted huskily. "After everything Carla did, I was determined I was never going to let myself love anyone again. But there was something about you…"

"I felt the same way about you," she said softly. "I was furious with you for suspecting me, but I couldn't get you out of my head. Then after the shop was broken into and you showed up just to see if I was okay, I knew I was in big trouble. You made me want things I didn't think I could have."

With a murmur of need, he kissed one corner of her mouth, then the other, little butterfly kisses that teased and seduced and promised so much more. "Tell me," he coaxed. "What do you want, sweetheart? Say the words."

She couldn't have denied him if her life had depended on it. Tears glistening in her eyes, she said, "I want you. I love you. I was afraid to, especially after you told me about Tommy. I knew you would want children, and I didn't think I could go there. Then everything turned upside down at Stacy's sonogram and then again, today, and I realized—"

Her throat suddenly tight with tears, she broke off abruptly, struggling for control. "I really do think I want a baby," she said huskily. "I know I'm probably going to be scared—"

"But that's what you have me for," he assured her. "And it's not something you have to rush into. I have

Tommy, and you two are going to be crazy about each other." He kissed her sweetly, fiercely. "I love you and all I want is for you to be happy."

"I am happy," she said huskily. "*You* make me happy."

"Marry me."

He hadn't meant to ask her like that, but the words just popped out. "I wasn't planning this today," he said ruefully. "I don't even have a ring. I should have waited and planned something romantic—"

"This is romantic."

"Standing outside a hospital nursery?" He chuckled.

"What hospital nursery? All I see is the man I love. That's all I need."

Touched, humbled, loving her more than he thought possible, he grinned. "I'm taking that as a yes, you know."

Her blue eyes dancing, she said, "I was hoping you would. Especially since you're going to be the father of my children."

He lifted a brow at that. "So now we've gone from having *a* baby to children. How many did you have in mind?"

"Well," she drawled, "I think that's open to discussion, don't you?"

"So convince me, sweetheart."

He expected her to give him a rational argument on why children needed siblings. Instead, she circled her arms around his neck and kissed him with a sweet, hot hunger that stole the breath right out of his lungs. When she finally let him up for air, he'd long since forgotten where they were.

"Well?" she asked huskily. "What do you think?"

"Six," he said hoarsely, and snatched her back, laughing, into his arms.

Epilogue

Everything was in its place. Icicle lights draped the windows and eaves, the Christmas tree was in its traditional place by the fireplace in the living room and the dining room table was overflowing with the food Kate O'Reilly had been preparing for the past three days. The New Year's Eve party was officially scheduled to start at eight, but no one had paid attention to that in years. The doorbell rang at seven, and within fifteen minutes, the house was packed to the rafters with friends and family who were in the mood to celebrate.

Dressed in a glistening red dress, her blue eyes sparkling like the diamonds at her ears, Mackenzie laughed as she was hugged and kissed by complete strangers who couldn't have been more thrilled for Patrick. He was pretty thrilled himself. Tommy was there, somewhere in the crowd, catching up with friends he hadn't seen in two years, and the woman he loved was within reach.

Grinning as his godfather, Neal Kennedy, gave Mackenzie a gentle kiss on the cheek, he stepped forward to claim his fiancée. "My turn," he said, and pulled a laughing Mackenzie under the mistletoe for a playfully lusty kiss.

Delighted, the crowd cheered.

"How about a toast?" Logan called out. "Devin, pass the champagne."

"I'm ready," he said and drew a laugh as he made his way through the crowd with an armful of champagne bottles. Other guests hurried forward to help with the serving, and within moments, the sea of glasses that were eagerly held up were filled.

When both Logan and Devin filled his and Mackenzie's glasses, Patrick chuckled. "I want pictures of this. My brothers are actually at my engagement party. Can you believe it? Has anyone checked outside? I think there's a herd of pigs flying over the house."

"Hey," Logan objected, making no effort to hold back a grin, "if I remember correctly, you burned your old marriage license right along with me and Devin and swore you were never going to get married again."

"True," he began, "but—"

"That was before he met me," Mackenzie quipped, her blue eyes dancing.

"That's right," Stacy added. Standing at Mackenzie's right, with John at her side, she grinned. "The poor man never had a chance. What's not to love?"

Chuckling, Patrick lifted a teasing brow at his brothers. "Well?"

"Nothing," Logan said quickly. "Absolutely nothing."

"That's right," Devin added with a grin. "You know we love you, Mac. If you had a sister—"

"You'd both be running for the hills," Kate O'Reilly quipped, smiling fondly at her two younger sons as the rest of the crowd laughed. Lifting her glass, she smiled joyfully at Patrick and Mackenzie. "To Patrick and Mackenzie. May their love and happiness last a lifetime."

The toast, accompanied by smiles and tears of happiness, echoed around the room, but Kate wasn't finished. "And," she added before the crowd could go back to celebrating, "to Logan and Devin."

"Whoa." Patrick laughed, caught off guard. "What's this? Why are we toasting these yo-yos?"

"Because they're next." Kate laughed and touched her glass to her sons'.

Stunned, Logan and Devin exchanged twin looks of panic. "Oh, God! We're doomed!"

* * * * *

*Celebrate 60 years of pure reading
pleasure with Harlequin®!
Just in time for the holidays,
Silhouette Special Edition®
is proud to present* New York Times
bestselling author Kathleen Eagle's
ONE COWBOY, ONE CHRISTMAS

Rodeo rider Zach Beaudry was a travelin' man—
until he broke down in middle-of-nowhere South
Dakota during a deep freeze. That's when an
angel came to his rescue....

"Don't die on me. Come on, Zel. You know how much I love you, girl. You're all I've got. Don't do this to me here. Not *now*."

But Zelda had quit on him, and Zach Beaudry had no one to blame but himself. He'd taken his sweet time hitting the road, and then miscalculated a shortcut. For all he knew he was a hundred miles from gas. But even if they were sitting next to a pump, the ten dollars he had in his pocket wouldn't get him out of South Dakota, which was not where he wanted to be right now. Not even his beloved pickup truck, Zelda, could get him much of anywhere on fumes. He was sitting out in the cold in the middle of nowhere. And getting colder.

He shifted the pickup into Neutral and pulled hard

on the steering wheel, using the downhill slope to get her off the blacktop and into the roadside grass, where she shuddered to a standstill. He stroked the padded dash. "You'll be safe here."

But Zach would not. It was getting dark, and it was already too damn cold for his cowboy ass. Zach's battered body was a barometer, and he was feeling South Dakota, big time. He'd have given his right arm to be climbing into a hotel hot tub instead of a brutal blast of north wind. The right was his free arm anyway. Damn thing had lost altitude, touched some part of the bull and caused him a scoreless ride last time out.

It wasn't scoring him a ride this night, either. A carload of teenagers whizzed by, topping off the insult by laying on the horn as they passed him. It was at least twenty minutes before another vehicle came along. He stepped out and waved both arms this time, damn near getting himself killed. Whatever happened to *do unto others?* In places like this, decent people didn't leave each other stranded in the cold.

His face was feeling stiff, and he figured he'd better start walking before his toes went numb. He struck out for a distant yard light, the only sign of human habitation in sight. He couldn't tell how distant, but he knew he'd be hurting by the time he got there, and he was counting on some kindly old man to be answering the door. No shame among the lame.

It wasn't like Zach was fresh off the operating table—it had been a few months since his last round of repairs—but he hadn't given himself enough time.

He'd lopped a couple of weeks off the near end of the doc's estimated recovery time, rigged up a brace, done some heavy-duty taping and climbed onto another bull. Hung in there for five seconds—four seconds past feeling the pop in his hip and three seconds short of the buzzer.

He could still feel the pain shooting down his leg with every step. Only this time he had to pick the damn thing up, swing it forward and drop it down again on his own.

Pride be damned, he just hoped *somebody* would be answering the door at the end of the road. The light in the front window was a good sign.

The four steps to the covered porch might as well have been four hundred, and he was looking to climb them with a lead weight chained to his left leg. His eyes were just as screwed up as his hip. Big black spots danced around with tiny red flashers, and he couldn't tell what was real and what wasn't. He stumbled over some shrubbery, steadied himself on the porch railing and peered between vertical slats.

There in the front window stood a spruce tree with a silver star affixed to the top. Zach was pretty sure the red sparks were all in his head, but the white lights twinkling by the hundreds throughout the huge tree, those were real. He wasn't too sure about the woman hanging the shiny balls. Most of her hair was caught up on her head and fastened in a curly clump, but the light captured by the escaped bits crowned her with a golden halo. Her face was a soft shadow, her body a willowy silhouette beneath a long white gown. If this was where the mind ran off to when cold started shutting down the rest of the body, then Zach's final worldly thought was, *This ain't such a bad way to go.*

If she would just turn to the window, he could die looking into the eyes of a Christmas angel.

* * * * *

Could this woman from Zach's past get the lonesome cowboy to come in from the cold...for good?
Look for
ONE COWBOY, ONE CHRISTMAS
by Kathleen Eagle.
Available December 2009 from
Silhouette Special Edition®.

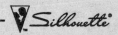

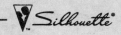

SPECIAL EDITION

**FROM *NEW YORK TIMES* AND *USA TODAY*
BESTSELLING AUTHOR**

KATHLEEN EAGLE

ONE COWBOY,
One Christmas

When bull rider Zach Beaudry appeared
out of thin air on Ann Drexler's ranch,
she thought she was seeing a ghost of
Christmas past. And though Zach had
no memory of their night of passion years
ago, they were about to share a future
he would never forget.

*Available December 2009
wherever books are sold.*

SSE65493

Visit Silhouette Books at www.eHarlequin.com

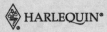

REQUEST YOUR FREE BOOKS!

2 FREE NOVELS PLUS 2 FREE GIFTS!

Silhouette® Romantic

SUSPENSE

Sparked by Danger, Fueled by Passion!

YES! Please send me 2 FREE Silhouette® Romantic Suspense novels and my 2 FREE gifts (gifts are worth about $10). After receiving them, if I don't wish to receive any more books, I can return the shipping statement marked "cancel." If I don't cancel, I will receive 4 brand-new novels every month and be billed just $4.24 per book in the U.S. or $4.99 per book in Canada. That's a savings of at least 15% off the cover price! It's quite a bargain! Shipping and handling is just 50¢ per book*. I understand that accepting the 2 free books and gifts places me under no obligation to buy anything. I can always return a shipment and cancel at any time. Even if I never buy another book from Silhouette, the two free books and gifts are mine to keep forever.

240 SDN EYL4   340 SDN EYMG

Name	(PLEASE PRINT)	
Address		Apt. #
City	State/Prov.	Zip/Postal Code

Signature (if under 18, a parent or guardian must sign)

Mail to the **Silhouette Reader Service:**
IN U.S.A.: P.O. Box 1867, Buffalo, NY 14240-1867
IN CANADA: P.O. Box 609, Fort Erie, Ontario L2A 5X3

Not valid to current subscribers of Silhouette Romantic Suspense books.

Want to try two free books from another line?
Call 1-800-873-8635 or visit www.morefreebooks.com.

* Terms and prices subject to change without notice. Prices do not include applicable taxes. Sales tax applicable in N.Y. Canadian residents will be charged applicable provincial taxes and GST. Offer not valid in Quebec. This offer is limited to one order per household. All orders subject to approval. Credit or debit balances in a customer's account(s) may be offset by any other outstanding balance owed by or to the customer. Please allow 4 to 6 weeks for delivery. Offer available while quantities last.

Your Privacy: Silhouette is committed to protecting your privacy. Our Privacy Policy is available online at www.eHarlequin.com or upon request from the Reader Service. From time to time we make our lists of customers available to reputable third parties who may have a product or service of interest to you. If you would prefer we not share your name and address, please check here. ☐

SRS09R

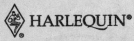

HARLEQUIN
Ambassadors

Want to share your passion for reading Harlequin® Books?

Become a Harlequin Ambassador!

Harlequin Ambassadors are a group of passionate and well-connected readers who are willing to share their joy of reading Harlequin® books with family and friends.

You'll be sent all the tools you need to spark great conversation, including free books!

All we ask is that you share the romance with your friends and family!

You'll also be invited to have a say in new book ideas and exchange opinions with women just like you!

To see if you qualify* to be a Harlequin Ambassador, please visit www.HarlequinAmbassadors.com.

*Please note that not everyone who applies to be a Harlequin Ambassador will qualify. For more information please visit www.HarlequinAmbassadors.com.

Thank you for your participation.

BAP09BPA

Romantic
SUSPENSE

COMING NEXT MONTH

Available November 24, 2009

#1587 THE CAVANAUGH CODE—Marie Ferrarella
Cavanaugh Justice
When detective Taylor McIntyre discovers a suspicious man lurking around a crime scene, she never guesses he'll be her new partner on the case. But the moment J. C. Laredo sweeps into the squad room, Taylor can't deny the attraction she feels for the P.I. As they work the nights away, growing ever closer to catching the killer, will they finally give in to the love that's been building inside?

#1588 THE SOLDIER'S SECRET DAUGHTER—Cindy Dees
Top Secret Deliveries
Her mystery man disappeared after their one night of passion, but he left Emily Grainger with a constant reminder—their daughter. So when she receives a tip that leads her to a ship's container, she's shocked to discover her long-lost love held captive inside! Now on the run from his captors, Jagger Holtz will do anything to protect his newly discovered family.

#1589 SEDUCED BY THE OPERATIVE—Merline Lovelace
Code Name: Danger
The president's daughter is having strange dreams, and psychologist Claire Cantwell has been tasked with finding their cause. In a desperate race against time, she and Colonel Luis Esteban follow a mysterious trail halfway around the world. As they face a lethal killer, can they also learn to face their own demons and give in to the love they clearly feel for each other?

#1590 PROTECTING THEIR BABY—Sheri WhiteFeather
Warrior Society
After her first and only one-night stand, Lisa Gordon suddenly finds herself pregnant...and in danger. Rex Sixkiller enjoys his free-spirited life, but when Lisa and his unborn child are threatened, he takes action. As the threats escalate and Rex fights to keep them safe, he and Lisa also wage a losing battle to protect their hearts.

SRSCNMBPA1109